ROCKY MOUNTAIN REVENGE

RHONDA STARNES

D0211748

LOVE INSPIRED SUSPENSE

INSPIRATIONAL ROMANCE

LOVE INSPIRED® SUSPENSE
INSPIRATIONAL ROMANCE

ISBN-13: 978-1-335-40295-0

Recycling programs for this product may not exist in your area.

Rocky Mountain Revenge

This edition published by arrangement with Harlequin Books S.A.

For questions and comments about the quality of this book, please contact us at CustomerService@Harlequin.com.

Love Inspired
22 Adelaide St. West, 40th Floor
Toronto, Ontario M5H 4E3, Canada
www.Harlequin.com

Printed in U.S.A.

And be ye kind one to another, tenderhearted, forgiving one another, even as God for Christ's sake hath forgiven you.

—Ephesians 4:32

For my husband, Coy, who told me to stop talking about "one day" and either write a book or shut up. You have always been my biggest cheerleader, and I would not have achieved this dream without you. Thank you for being my happily-ever-after.

For my children and grandchildren. You are my greatest blessings. I love you forever!

For my dad, I'm so thankful you and Mom raised me to work hard and never give up. My biggest regret is not chasing this dream sooner, so Mom would have been here to celebrate.

Also, special thanks to:

My editor, Tina James, for making my dream of being a Love Inspired Suspense author come true and for helping me teach my students that hard work pays off.

Connie Queen, for asking me if I wanted to be critique partners six years ago. What a journey it has been. We made it!

Tina Radcliffe, for your guidance and wisdom and for encouraging me when I grew weary.

My writing sisters and critique partners, for your encouragement, support and prayers.

My family, friends and students for cheering me on.

ONE

Grace Porter regretted she hadn't stopped for fuel before leaving Denver two hours ago, when it was still daylight. If she had, she wouldn't be at a run-down gas station that looked like it belonged in a low-budget horror movie. A dim yellow light flickered overhead and made a strange buzzing sound. The attendant, a tall, gaunt man with oily brown hair, stood behind the counter and stared at her through the window, reminding her of Norman Bates.

At least the two pumps had been updated to the pay-at-the-pump variety, so she wouldn't have to go inside.

She pulled the nozzle out of the car's gas tank, settled it back on its cradle and drummed her fingers on the side of her red Honda CRV as she waited for the receipt to print. Though she wasn't typically scared of shadows in the dark, the overcast night sky obscured the moon and stars, providing little visibility outside the immediate rim of the artificial light from the gas station awning. A light breeze made the already cool late-May night air even colder, sending a shiver up her arms.

Why was she feeling uneasy? She'd filled up her car at this very station numerous times when she was younger, often late at night when heading home from a friend's house. Had living in Denver the past eight years made her dependent on streetlights on every corner for a sense of security?

Hopefully, she would only be in Blackberry Falls for a couple of months then she could return to her life in Denver. In the meantime, she would provide emotional support to her sister, Chloe, as she finalized her divorce. She would also have to focus on hiring someone to replace James, her soon-to-be ex-brother-in-law, as the veterinarian at the animal clinic she and Chloe had inherited two years ago.

Grace had never wanted to be a small-town veterinarian, but here she was about to temporarily take over the reins of the clinic her father had built. Something he'd always wanted but she'd always tried to avoid.

Chloe couldn't be expected to continue working with James until a replacement could be found. It had been difficult enough for her sister to continue going to work as the clinic's office manager the past few months while Grace worked out the details of her leave of absence from the animal hospital in Denver where she worked as a veterinary cardiologist.

Grace didn't understand her sister's emotional attachment to their hometown and would have suggested Chloe walk away and start fresh in a new city if she thought her words would have been welcomed.

She startled at the sudden blare of music emanating from her vehicle. Chloe's ringtone. Grace tore off the receipt, shoved it into the back pocket of her jeans and slid behind the steering wheel. Grabbing her phone off the dashboard, she slid a finger across the screen, silencing Sister Sledge in the middle of "We Are Family." Her sister's face filled the screen.

"Chloe. Why are you FaceTiming? What if I were driving?"

Chloe's blue eyes sparkled. "I checked the app and saw that you had stopped for gas."

"Then you also saw I'm only ten minutes away." Grace smiled.

"I know, but I got held up at the clinic and just arrived home."

Chloe had always hated going into an empty house by herself after dark. When she couldn't avoid doing that, she would call Grace to video chat as she entered the house, claiming it made her feel less alone. Her theory was that Grace could call 9-1-1 if there was an intruder.

This was getting out of hand. Maybe, while Grace was back in Blackberry Falls, she could finally get Chloe to install an alarm system and sign up for self-defense classes.

Grace sighed. "Okay. But be fast."

Chloe exited her vehicle. "Man, it's dark out here tonight. Good thing you gave me this flashlight key chain for Christmas last year. It's the only reason I haven't tripped and busted my face."

Her sister never would have stayed out late on such a dark night if she could have helped it. "What kept you at the clinic so late?"

"We can discuss that after you get here. Oh, but I do need to tell you, I received another letter from Benjamin Hamilton wanting to purchase the farm."

The farm was eighty acres of prime pastureland and the two-story farmhouse they had lived in growing up. It had sat empty since their father died, until Chloe moved back in several months ago. Grace had no need of the property and planned to sign over her share to Chloe once her divorce was finalized.

"Didn't you tell him you plan to live there permanently?"

"I did. His recent letter lists all the reasons I shouldn't live out here alone." Keys jingled. "Hang on a second while I open the door."

The screen went black. "Chloe, I can't see you. The screen says 'Poor Connection.'"

A thud boomed across the line, and her sister's scream split the air. "No! No-o-o!"

Grace's heart pounded. The video reconnected, but the ceiling had replaced her sister's image.

"Chloe. Are you okay? What's happening?" Grace yelled into the phone.

Had Chloe's Great Dane, Barkley, knocked her down?

"Chloe! Answer me. Right now."

The sound of a struggle and furniture being knocked over echoed in the background. "Okay, I'm calling nine-one-one."

A person wearing a full-face novelty ski mask that resembled a black bear stared into the phone. Brown eyes glared at her, assessing.

An involuntary gasp escaped Grace's lips as she covered her mouth with a trembling hand.

"Go ahead. It'll be too late by the time they get here." He laughed and the screen went blank.

Pressing the call button on the steering wheel, she put the vehicle into gear and sped out of the parking lot.

"Nine-one-one. What's your emergency?"

"My sister." Grace took the curve at Newfound Gap fast. Too fast. Except right now there was no such thing as too fast. "Chloe Osborne, 1362 Monteagle Lane. Someone broke in. I heard a struggle and a scream. There's a masked man, and the phone went blank."

"There's an intruder?"

Wasn't that what she'd said? Grace bit back angry

words and fought to stay calm. "Yes—1362 Monteagle Lane."

The dispatcher repeated the address. Then, "What is your name?"

What did that matter? Why weren't they sending a troop of police cars, lights flashing and sirens screaming, to Chloe's house?

The nearest neighbors are a half mile away. There's no one to hear my sister's cries for help.

"Ma'am, your name?"

"Grace. Dr. Grace Porter. Chloe's my sister. Why aren't you sending help?"

"Help is on the way."

The dispatcher's calm voice infuriated Grace. Chloe's life was in danger! How could she be so absolutely nonchalant?

She's supposed to be calm. That's why she's got this job. Breathe. Think. Pray.

But she couldn't breathe. Not normally. Or think. The only thing she could envision was Chloe's worst nightmare coming true. Being on the phone with Grace hadn't stopped it from happening.

Disconnecting the call, she pressed harder on the accelerator.

Please, Lord, let help arrive in time.

She turned onto the road that led to her childhood home and pulled up to the edge of the property, cutting the engine. Even from this distance, she could see the front door was open. Lights spilled out from the downstairs windows.

Now what? There was no sign of the police yet.

She couldn't sit there. Her sister might be injured. Or worse—dead.

What could she use as a weapon?

Digging through the glove compartment, she found a flashlight, an ice scraper and the vehicle owner's manual.

Ugh, what else do I have?

She felt under the passenger seat. An umbrella. Success!

Thankful for the cover of darkness, she sprinted across the lawn. Reaching the corner of the two-story farmhouse, she inched along the side, stopping at every window to peek and listen.

A whimpering growl sounded. She pressed her face against the cool glass of the window. Barkley, locked in a bedroom, clawed at the door. Desperate to save his owner. Grace's veterinarian heart bled for him, but she couldn't offer comforting words for fear he'd reveal her presence.

She reached the porch and climbed. One. Step. At. A. Time.

Muffled voices reached her. Chloe's and a man's. Deep and guttural.

Umbrella at the ready, she entered the house and stopped short. Chloe, her back to the stairs, was struggling with her attacker on the second-floor landing.

The faint sound of a siren pierced the night.

Thank you, Lord.

The masked man met her eyes above Chloe's head, and for a split second, she wondered if she'd spoken the words out loud.

Inching closer to the stairs, Grace battled the desire to race up to them. If she distracted her sister from her mission of survival, it could be catastrophic. Chloe must have sensed her presence because she glanced over her shoulder. That was all the edge the attacker needed.

He pushed Chloe, and her body bent backward over the railing. She had one hand gripping the wood rail, the other grasping his mask.

Grace charged. Before she made it even midway up the curved staircase, her sister flew through the air.

"Chloe!"

She landed on the foyer floor in a heap, a ski mask in her outstretched hand.

Grace rushed down. Footsteps pounded on the stairs right behind her. She looked over her shoulder. A man in his midforties, with collar-length brown hair and a scruffy beard sprinkled with gray, smirked at her.

She raised the umbrella to ward off an attack. The man ducked and head-butted her in the side, sending her tumbling down the last four steps.

Pushing herself up onto her hands and knees, she pressed a hand against the wall, struggling to stand.

The man snickered as he planted his booted foot on her back and pushed her flat to the floor. "You're next, Amazing Grace."

She froze. *Amazing Grace. She hadn't heard that name in two years, not since her father died. How did he know Dad's nickname for her?*

Sirens grew louder as red-and-blue strobe lights bounced across the walls. The man sprinted out of sight. Seconds later, she heard the kitchen door, leading into the backyard, bang closed.

Grasping the newel post, she pulled herself to her feet and raced to Chloe, who lay crumpled on her side like a discarded rag doll. A pool of blood seeped out from under her head.

Chloe's breathing was shallow. Grace bent and checked for a pulse. Weak. Placing her hands on either side of Chloe's neck, she pressed in gently with her fingers and ran them up the length of the neck to the base of the head. It did not appear to be broken. Carefully, tilting her sister's head, Grace examined the wound. A bump had already appeared, in the center of which was a gash about two inches long. It didn't seem very deep, but would require stitches.

Grabbing a chunky, knit cardigan off the hook near the door, she knelt beside her sister and applied pressure to the wound. "Hang in there, sis. Help is on the way."

Childhood memories swarmed her as Dad's constant reminder echoed in her mind. *Amazing Grace, as the big sister, it's your job to take care of Chloe.*

Footsteps sounded on the porch. An officer entered the house, gun at the ready. "Are there more intruders?"

Her head snapped in his direction. Hazel eyes pierced hers. Grace's breath caught. She hadn't expected *him* to respond.

"Grace. How many intruders?" Chief Evan Bradshaw's question came out harsher than he intended, but he needed to assess the situation and was barely holding himself back from rushing to her side.

She shook her head. "Only one. He went out the back."

"We saw him. Johnson took off after him." Evan holstered his weapon. "How badly is she hurt?"

"Head wound. Her pulse is weak. Possible internal injuries. Won't know for sure until she has some scans." Grace's voice cracked, and he knew she was struggling to keep her composure.

"Where's the ambulance?" Desperation echoed in her voice. Blue eyes pleaded with him, tears pooling.

Evan clenched his hands at his sides, fighting the urge to pull her into a hug, the way he would have when they were younger.

Instead, he knelt beside her, taking a quick assessment. Grace held a cloth of some sort against Chloe's head. There was a lot of blood, but he knew that wasn't uncommon for head wounds. "She'll be okay, Gracie. I promise."

Now, why had he said that? Who was he to make promises? He'd learned a long time ago he couldn't stop death. Losing his unborn daughter and his wife three months apart had taught him that.

Chloe's pale face stood out in stark contrast against the bloodstained rug. He watched for the rise and fall of her chest, as he had his now six-year-old son, Camden, when he was an infant. Chloe's breathing was almost imperceptible, but it was steady.

"What's taking the ambulance so long?" Grace wiped her face, silent tears flowing freely now. "I can't lose her."

From the moment they'd met in sixth grade until high school graduation, Evan and Grace had been inseparable. During that time, he had only seen her cry twice. The first time in seventh grade when her cat, Mitzi, died. The second, the summer before their sophomore year of high school when her mom died from cancer. Her crying now meant she'd started to lose hope that Chloe would survive.

He needed to keep Grace busy so her mind didn't wander down the what-if trail. "Go find a blanket. We need to keep her warm until the ambulance arrives."

Her eyes widened. "Shock. Why didn't I think of that?" Tilting Chloe's head so the floor would hold the cloth in place, she crossed the foyer into the living room.

While she did as he asked, Evan used his phone to snap a few photos of Chloe's position. Two of his officers were en route. They'd take additional shots of the perimeter and interior of the house.

Grace returned with a fuzzy, paisley-print throw. She draped it across her sister's body then ran her bloodstained hands along the length of Chloe's arms and legs.

"Nothing appears to be broken, but we won't know for sure until she has X-rays."

"Can you tell me what happened?"

"We were on video chat." Her voice shook.

She closed her eyes and took a deep breath. Then her lips moved in silent prayer, something he hadn't done in a long time. He guessed it was some comfort that she could cling to her faith when in distress.

"Take your time."

She met his eyes; her gaze steady, tears gone. "He told me calling nine-one-one wouldn't do any good. Help would arrive too late."

"Who told you?"

"The man who did this. Before he disconnected the call."

Evan's gut tightened. The attacker had seen Grace. He wished he could spare her the questions but knew he couldn't. "Did you see his face?"

"Not then…but when he pushed Chloe over the banister, she pulled off his ski mask." Grace nodded to the black fabric in Chloe's outstretched hand.

How had he missed seeing this important piece of evidence?

Get your head into the game, Bradshaw. Don't let Grace's presence throw you. You're not a lovesick teen any longer.

Turning back to her, he asked, "Did you recognize the attacker?"

"No."

She shivered, and once again, he clenched his hands. Why did he think he had to touch her to comfort her? He'd always strove to be compassionate to victims and witnesses, but he'd never wanted to embrace one before. The way he did her. Could the instinct simply be a muscle memory?

"He knew me." Her whisper was barely audible.

Evan's gut tightened. "What did you say?"

"Chloe's attacker knew me. He called me Amazing Grace."

Dr. Porter had been the only one to call his daughter Amazing Grace. Even Evan had never called her by that nickname, respecting the bond she had with her dad.

"He said I was next," she whispered.

Evan bit back an exclamation. He couldn't allow her to see that her words had shaken him.

The dying wail of a siren announced the arrival of the ambulance.

A dog howled from somewhere deep within the house.

"Barkley," Grace said. "I forgot all about him. He's locked in the master bedroom."

Two EMTs entered the house wearing trauma–jump bag backpacks. Evan gave a silent signal to let them know they could take care of the victim but couldn't move anything.

Lieutenant Johnson entered the house right behind the medics. He met Evan's eyes and gave a slight shake of his head. Suspect not apprehended.

Pulling Grace away from Chloe, Evan whispered, "Give them room to work." He turned her to face him and jerked his head toward the hall. The sound of Chloe's dog's whimpering grew louder. "Why don't you go check on Barkley?"

"But…" She looked from him to Chloe and back again, the internal struggle etched on her face.

"Go. You're the vet. Make sure Barkley is okay." He smiled. Encouraging her to trust him. "I'll stay here. Chloe won't leave my sight."

The medics spoke in low tones behind them. Checking vitals. Making decisions.

Grace nodded, a wisp of blond hair falling in her face. His hand froze in midair. Another muscle memory. He let his hand drop to his side. He didn't have the right to brush hair out of her face. And hadn't in fifteen years, not since the day of high school graduation when she'd decided Evan and Blackberry Falls weren't enough for her. "Go on. I'll let you know when they're ready to transport her."

Grace wiped away a tear, offered him a shaky smile of thanks and then turned and went down the hall.

As soon as she was out of range, he snapped more photos with his cell phone and bagged the ski mask. Rage reverberated through him when he saw the image screen-printed on the fleece mask. Being attacked was brutal. Being attacked by someone looking like a black bear seemed extra cruel.

He nodded to the stocky, bald medic. Patterson, according to his name badge. "How bad is she?"

"Critical."

"Please, save her."

"That's always our goal, man." Patterson inclined his head toward the outdoors. "How well do you know this area? I need a place for my medical transport pilot to land."

"There's a hay field, past the barn, about a hundred and fifty feet behind the house."

"That'll work."

"Two officers are arriving on scene now. I'll have them park where their headlights illuminate the area."

Evan radioed his officers as the EMTs worked to stabilize Chloe. Then he pulled Johnson aside.

"Where'd the guy go?"

"I'm not sure, boss. I chased him through the woods and across the creek that borders the Hamilton Thoroughbred Ranch before I lost him. He took off in an old black truck."

"I can't imagine the Hamiltons allowing just anyone to park on their property. You think he works for them?"

"I don't know, but he knew the terrain, giving him an advantage over me."

"Did you go up to the main house and talk to Ben?"

"I did. It took several minutes to get someone to the door. Ben said he and Mrs. Hamilton were watching a movie in the basement, so he hadn't heard any vehicles leaving the property."

"Surely you described the truck to him. Did he have any idea who it could belong to?"

His lieutenant shook his head. "He said, and I quote, 'If I spent all my time trying to keep track of my employees' vehicles, I wouldn't have time to run my ranch.'"

Evan bit back a retort as Grace walked toward him. A massive fawn-colored Great Dane trailed behind her, the top of his head almost reaching her shoulder. The animal easily outweighed her by seventy pounds or more. It was a sight to behold.

"This must be Barkley," Evan said.

The medic who was kneeling beside Chloe moved, and before anyone could stop the dog, he walked over to his mistress and put his nose to her chest. Grace whistled, and the animal ambled back to her side.

"I couldn't keep him contained any longer. He needed to see her." She shrugged. "So did I."

"It's okay," Evan replied. "I was about to come get you. They're getting ready to transport her to Denver Memorial."

"Denver? That's over two hours away." She didn't take

her eyes off the medical team as they secured Chloe to a stretcher, an IV already pushing vital fluids through her veins. "Wouldn't County be closer?"

"Denver Memorial is one of the best trauma hospitals in the state." The house rumbled as the air ambulance helicopter flew overhead.

"I want to go with her. Make them take me with her." She clutched his arm, her voice pleading.

Evan shook his head. His chest tightened at the pain in her eyes. "Gracie, they don't have enough room to take passengers. Besides, we've got to take care of Barkley before we leave."

"But…"

"I'll get you to Denver. Fast. You'll be the first person to see her after the doctors have run all their tests."

"What if *he* gets to her first?" Her shoulders slumped.

Unable to resist, he pulled her into a tight embrace. He would regret it later. But she was hurting, and for now, he was the only one she had to lean on. "He won't. I promise."

"How can you promise that?" She spoke into his chest. "Denver is outside your jurisdiction."

Evan pulled back and looked down at her. He didn't care what it took. Even if he had to pay for a private security guard himself, he would not let her down. "I promise. She will have a guard twenty-four seven until her attacker has been caught." *And so will you.*

TWO

Grace stepped out of Evan's arms, avoiding eye contact. Her cheeks warmed. Why had he pulled her into an embrace? More importantly, why had she allowed him to? Because she had been worried about Chloe. No other reason. He had only been offering comfort in a time of distress. A perfectly normal reaction. Almost half of her life had been lived since walking away from him the day he proposed. She had moved on. So had he.

After she moved to Fort Collins for college and then settled in Denver, Chloe and Dad had made it their mission in life to keep her up-to-date on current events in Blackberry Falls, including Evan getting married, becoming a father and then losing his wife.

The embrace had simply been an old friend offering comfort. Nothing more.

"Logroll to the left on three. One…two…three."

The commanding voice penetrated Grace's foggy brain and the activity around her came into focus.

"Okay, guys, let's move."

"No. Wait!" She pushed past Evan and chased after the medics carrying Chloe out of the house. Racing down the steps of the porch, she touched the arm of the medic at the head of the backboard. "One minute. Please."

He nodded. "One minute."

Grace brushed Chloe's light brown hair out of her face. She longed to see her sister's laughing, blue eyes, but they remained closed. "I'll be at the hospital as soon as I get Barkley taken care of. I love you, sis." She gently kissed Chloe's forehead and stepped back. *Please, Lord, let her be okay.*

The medics continued toward the helicopter. She jogged alongside them until a strong hand pulled her back at the edge of the field.

Turning, she met Evan's eyes. No point asking if she could drive herself to the hospital. She had enough sense to know she shouldn't travel alone, not after she'd seen the attacker's face. "How soon can we leave?"

"I need to give Johnson a few instructions." He nodded at the Great Dane at her side. "What are you going to do with him?"

"We'll take him to the clinic. If there's no room in the kennel, I'll leave him in the apartment upstairs. If I'm not back by morning, I can have one of the staff feed and walk him." She sighed. "As a matter of fact, I probably need to take my car and leave my stuff there. Then I won't have to come back here."

A look flashed in his eyes, as if he might argue, but he didn't. "Get whatever Barkley needs. I'll be ready when you're finished."

"Five minutes. That's all I need." She ran her hand over the dog's back. "Come on, boy."

True to his word, Evan was ready to go as soon as she returned. She quickly loaded Barkley into the backseat of her Honda CRV and pulled out of the drive. Evan followed behind in his gray department-issued SUV with the Blackberry Falls PD logo emblazoned on the side.

Ten minutes later, she pulled into the employee parking area at the side of Porter Animal Clinic, an old stone-and-cedar building on the edge of town. The structure had evolved over the nearly forty years of its existence, expanding to more than three times its original size. The sight of the business her father built through hard work and dedication brought a flood of emotions. She thought of Dad every single day. Had it only been two years since that automobile accident had taken his life? Seemed much longer. Grief compressed her heart, squeezing her chest. Would she lose Chloe, too?

Grace had barely put the vehicle into Park when Evan tapped on her window. "Don't cut the engine."

"What? Why?"

"I need to check the area to make sure no one is lurking around or waiting inside." He slipped his gun out of its holster. "I want you outta here fast if something happens."

Grace's mouth went dry. Her throat tightened, making it impossible to get words out. She hadn't even thought about the possibility the attacker could be waiting for her here.

"It'll be okay. Keep your doors locked and the engine running. If I'm not back in ten minutes, get out of here. Go straight to the station. Got it?"

She nodded agreement.

Thankful Chloe had always insisted she have easy access to the clinic they co-owned even if she didn't work there, Grace handed him keys and wrote down the pass codes to the security system and the lock on the apartment door. Then she rolled up her window and watched as he entered the darkened building.

What on earth had she come home to? Her breath caught and tears stung her eyes. *Lord, please let Chloe be okay. Don't let me lose my sister like this.*

She took some steadying breaths. It wouldn't help

Chloe for her to fall apart. The only thing she could do for her sister at this moment was to help figure out the identity of their attacker. Why had he attacked Chloe in the first place? She was fairly certain the guy hadn't been a robber caught off guard when the homeowner returned. If he had been, why had he threatened Grace? Even calling her by her childhood nickname. She'd been distracted enough when Chloe had fallen. He could have taken the back stairs down to the kitchen and escaped without her seeing his face.

To her knowledge, her sister didn't have any enemies. Was this connected to the clinic? If it was, why had the man said she was next in a way that made it seem like that had always been his plan and wasn't just because she'd seen his face? Other than being a silent partner, Grace had nothing to do with the clinic.

Did this have something to do with Chloe and James's divorce? Grace had a hard time believing James would want to harm Chloe. He'd always seemed so devoted to her…but apparently things were not always as they seemed on the surface. He'd put her sister through so much anguish.

Should she call him to tell him about the attack? Legally, he was Chloe's husband, at least for another week until the divorce was finalized. Maybe Evan could advise her about contacting him.

A shiver racked her body. She rubbed her arms and took concentrated breaths. Needing to do something constructive, she dug into her purse and pulled out a pen and an old receipt. She flipped the receipt over and jotted down details about the attacker as they flashed in her mind.

Midforties. Brown eyes. Dark brown hair—collar-length, wavy, some graying. Oblong face. Cleft chin.

Height? Hmm. This one was harder. The man had been standing at the top of the stairs. Though, he hadn't seemed much more than half a foot taller than Chloe's five-four frame.

To the list, she added "five-ten" followed by a question mark.

Grace tapped the pen on the steering wheel and glanced at the dashboard. Eleven thirty-seven. Evan had been inside nine minutes. Where was he? She peered through the windshield. The clinic had never seemed scary before, but tonight she noticed the shadowed areas around the building. She'd have additional lighting installed the first chance she got.

Dogs barked in the kennel that connected to the back of the building and ran parallel to the parking area. Someone moved along the perimeter inside the fence. Her breath caught, then she exhaled. Evan. She'd recognize his confident stride anywhere.

Evan was a good man, hardworking and loyal. She wasn't surprised when he'd been promoted to chief of police at the young age of thirty, the youngest in Blackberry Falls' history. He had always been a planner; when he set goals, he reached them.

When he'd proposed to her the night they'd graduated high school, he'd had their whole life planned. They would attend Colorado State University Pueblo, each taking a hefty course load to complete their bachelor degrees in three years. After graduation, Evan would attend the police academy and Grace would transfer to Colorado State University in Fort Collins to complete her Doctor of Veterinary Medicine PhD, which would have meant a long-distance relationship for four years. They'd marry after she graduated and settle in Blackberry Falls. Though she'd loved him deeply and had dreamed of a life with him, it had all seemed a bit too much to her eighteen-year-old self. She'd bolted.

Would things have been different if she had agreed to return to Blackberry Falls and marry him? One thing was for sure, if she had returned home, Dad wouldn't have hired James and Chloe wouldn't have gone through the heartache and disappointment he'd put her through the past few years.

What else would have been different? Would Chloe still have been attacked tonight? Would Grace be afraid for her life?

Evan slipped back into the clinic and closed the door, muffling the sound of the barking. He'd cleared the interior and exterior. No signs of an intruder, at least not one still hanging around. There were a couple of areas of concern, namely an unlocked exterior door and an office behind the reception area that looked like it may have been ransacked. Either that or the person who the office belonged to was a bit of a slob.

He flipped on the hall light and headed for the side entrance to get Grace and Chloe's miniature-horse-size dog. They needed to get the Great Dane settled quickly and be on their way to the hospital.

His cell phone vibrated with a text message from his former high school football teammate. Ryan Vincent was a co-owner of the private security firm Protective Instincts. Evan had called him on the drive to the clinic and requested his assistance.

At hospital. I'm stationed outside Chloe's ER room. Bridget is in waiting area on lookout. See you when you get here.

Evan wasn't sure how Ryan had received permission to enter the examination area of the ER, but he was thankful to have a friend with those kinds of connections.

He typed a quick reply.

10-4. Thanks. ETA 2 hours.

If I exceed the speed limit and don't run into any trouble.

For Grace's sake, he needed to make the trip as quickly as possible. Or was it for his sake? The ride could get awkward. They hadn't spent more than a few minutes in each other's presence since the day of high school graduation. Not that he had any lingering feelings for her. He had grown up and realized a childhood love rarely manifested into a lifelong, lasting relationship. He'd moved on, discovering Grace had made the right decision by not marrying him. If Evan had learned one thing from his marriage, it was that he wasn't marriage material. Now a widower and single father of a six-year-old boy, he'd likely remain single.

Camden. His son was a blessing. Thankfully, he was spending the night with his maternal grandparents.

Evan exited the building and found Grace standing at the back of her SUV, Barkley at her side. The cargo liftgate was open.

"What are you doing out of the vehicle?" He increased his stride and reached her side in time to lift the large suitcase out of the back.

"I'm unloading the necessities." She shrugged. "I saw the light come on, so I figured all was safe."

He scrubbed his hand across his face. "Still. You should have waited on me."

"I knew you were on your way out, and we're in a hurry. We need to get to the hospital ASAP."

He couldn't argue with that, but he'd have to find a way to make her understand the seriousness of the situation. She was a target.

Evan sighed. In a few minutes, they were going to be inside a vehicle for a two-hour drive. He'd wait until then to hammer home the facts and how she had to follow his instructions if she wanted to stay safe.

"Get the dog. I've got the bag." He closed the liftgate and ushered her into the building. "As far as I could tell, both the indoor and outdoor kennels looked full."

Animals barked and meowed in the far reaches of the clinic, masking their footsteps on the old tile floors. If he hadn't already cleared the building, he'd be concerned someone could sneak up on them in this environment.

"That's okay. It's probably best to leave Barkley in the apartment. It'll feel more like home." Grace started up the stairs, and he touched her arm and halted her.

"About that. The exterior door to the apartment was unlocked when I went in. Maybe no one thought physically locking it was important since there's a digital door lock. But that's not the case. While it's convenient not having to dig out a key, digital locks are easily hacked."

Surprise registered on her face, and her eyes widened. "It should have been locked. We always use both the key and the code to enter the exterior door."

"The apartment looked undisturbed. I'll need you to do a quick check, though, to be sure nothing is missing."

They entered the small one-bedroom apartment, and Grace did a hurried walk-through. "Nothing seems to be missing, but I can't be positive. It's been almost two years since I last stayed here."

That would mean she hadn't been home since Andrew

Porter had died. Though he'd rarely run into Grace when she'd come to Blackberry Falls, it surprised him it had been so long since she'd visited. Maybe coming home after losing her dad had been too painful.

Evan probably understood the pain of loss better than anyone. It had been difficult for him to return home after his wife had been murdered. Beautiful, compassionate Lisa. He'd felt the loss of her presence everywhere in town. Eventually, he learned to avoid the painful places. Even finding excuses not to attend church, where he missed her sweet, soprano voice and the feel of her hand in his during prayer in the early years of their marriage. Before she'd slipped into depression.

He'd let Lisa down as a husband and as a protector. Most days, he barely stayed a step ahead of the wave of guilt that threatened to drown him.

There would be no way to outrun the tsunami that would engulf him if he failed to protect Gracie, too.

Grace filled Barkley's water bowl and placed it a few feet from his dog bed. "All done. Let's get to the hospital."

It had been an hour since the air ambulance had transported Chloe to Memorial, and Grace was anxious to get to the ER to see if her sister was awake. She also wanted to question the doctor about Chloe's condition.

Evan motioned for her to lead the way down the stairs and back through the clinic. "I need you to check one more room before we leave."

She half turned on the stairs to look at him, raising an eyebrow. What had he found on his walk-through?

"The office tucked in the corner behind the receptionist desk looks like it may have been ransacked. Or the person it belongs to is unorganized and messy."

Grace pressed her lips together to suppress the laughter bubbling up inside her.

"What's so funny?" Evan looked at her like she'd lost her mind.

Nothing. Nothing at all. Sadness washed over her. Chloe's messiness had been a family joke for years.

She took a few steadying breaths. "That's Chloe's office. Unorganized and messy is her nature. I'll look, but I can almost guarantee the mess has Chloe written all over it."

He led her to her sister's office, stopping her in the doorway. "Don't touch anything until you're sure it's the way Chloe would have left it."

She nodded. "Sure. No prob—"

The front door of the clinic burst open, and Evan pushed her into the office, turning to block her as he pulled his gun.

"What is going on?" James Osborne's voice boomed. "Why are you prowling around my clinic, chief?"

"First, it's not *your* clinic. Second, I'm not prowling."

"Oh, really. Then why did several of the neighbors call to tell me someone was skulking through the kennels, upsetting the dogs?"

Grace tamped down the anger that threatened. The busybodies of Blackberry Falls were at it again. If any of those neighbors had looked closely, they would have seen it was the police chief's SUV in the parking lot and not an intruder's. Or maybe they had noticed and were looking to start the gossip mill. She sighed and slipped further out of sight. At least she no longer had to figure out whether or not to notify James about the night's events.

Evan holstered his weapon and walked into the reception area, his footsteps echoing on the tile floor.

"There was an incident at the farm this evening. Grace and I thought it best to bring Barkley here."

"What? Where's Chloe?"

Thankful Evan was the one dealing with James, she turned and looked at her sister's office, tuning out the conversation in the reception area.

A raincoat, two Porter Animal Clinic T-shirts and an oversize tote bag covered the filing cabinet in the corner. It looked more like forgotten exercise equipment in someone's bedroom than an important piece of office furniture. In typical Chloe fashion, files that should have been in the cabinet were stacked in multiple piles on the desk. Even with modern technology, her sister preferred to work with paper copies. Once accounts were settled, she knew Chloe scanned copies into the computer and shredded the originals. A few files she'd obviously been working on before leaving work for the day lay open, contents scattered across her closed laptop. Could the laptop hold answers to Chloe's attack?

When Chloe had called to tell her about her marriage problems, she'd also mentioned that some things at the clinic hadn't been adding up lately. Hence, Grace taking a leave of absence and returning home to take over the clinic from James while they searched for a replacement.

The men's footsteps drew closer. Grabbing the tote bag off the cabinet, she quickly shoved the folders and the laptop into it. Then she noticed a file without a label peeking out from under the desk blotter. She shoved it into the bag, slipped the strap over her shoulder and turned, making eye contact with Evan as he and James entered the room. He glanced at the tote and raised an eyebrow. She prayed he wouldn't ask about the bag and James would think it was just her oversize purse.

"Grace!" James pushed past Evan and came to stand

in front of her. Gray eyes looked at her accusingly. "Why didn't you call to tell me someone attacked Chloe and she was injured?"

She took a deep breath, releasing it before answering. "I wasn't sure of proper protocol since she's your ex-wife...or she will be after next week."

"I realize that." He shoved a hand through his short, chestnut-colored hair. "It doesn't mean I don't want to know what's happening to her."

"I'm sorry. I had planned to call you once we left here. Chloe and Barkley had to be my primary focus."

"Of course. You're right. The main thing is I know now. So, come on. I'll drive you to the hospital, and we'll find out how she is." He grasped her wrist and dragged her toward the door.

Grace pulled free, stepping back and bumping against the desk. She rubbed her wrist.

James turned and took a step in her direction.

"Whoa." Evan blocked his path. "As Grace pointed out, you're in the middle of a divorce. There's no reason for you to go to the hospital. I'll take her as planned."

"But—"

"No, James." She offered a sympathetic smile. After all he'd put her sister through, Grace never would have thought she'd ever feel sorry for James. "Evan's right. I know you don't automatically stop caring about someone because the relationship is over. But you no longer have the right to be by their side when they're injured or in pain."

For the second time in as many hours, she avoided Evan's eyes, remembering how she'd had to restrain herself from driving down to check on him a few times in the past fifteen years—most recently, four years ago when she'd heard of his wife's murder. He'd been her childhood best friend, and a part of her would always want to know he was okay. But, like James, that hadn't given her the right to be where she wasn't needed. Or wanted.

She touched his arm. "I'll let you know how she is. I promise."

"Okay. I'll be at home, waiting for your call."

"Actually," Evan interjected, "I'd like you to stop by the station first."

"What? Why?"

"I need you to give a statement."

James paled. "You can't think I was the one who attacked Chloe."

"No. I sa—" Grace swallowed the rest of her words when Evan squeezed her hand and gave a subtle shake of his head.

"I'm an upstanding member of this community." Anger flashed in James's eyes as his voice rose. "Just because my wife decided she didn't want to be married any longer doesn't mean I'd want to kill her."

His words struck her like a sharp jab to the solar plexus. Chloe had told her about James's temper, but she'd never seen a hint of it before now. He had always been soft-spoken and mild-mannered.

"Look. I'm not accusing you of anything. It's standard practice to interview the husband, especially if the parties are in the middle of a divorce." Evan's tone softened like he was talking to a buddy. "Honestly, I fully expect your alibi to check out. What I'm really hoping is that you can offer some insight into who might be behind the attack."

James's jaw twitched. After a long pause, he conceded. "Okay."

They all exited the building and locked up. As they turned to leave, Evan clapped James on the back. "I'll call Lieutenant Johnson and let him know to expect you."

James opened his mouth, then closed it. He looked as if he still wanted to argue, but he nodded, climbed into his vehicle and sped away.

Evan opened the door for Grace. She settled into the passenger seat of the police SUV, thankful there was room for her up front so she didn't have to ride in the backseat like a prisoner. Then he jogged around the front of the vehicle, slid behind the steering wheel, started the engine and backed out of the parking lot.

"Okay Gracie, now that we're alone, why don't you tell me what's in the bag besides the file I saw you swipe?"

THREE

"I'll answer all of your questions," Grace said. "After I call the hospital to check on Chloe."

"Do you think they'll tell you anything over the phone?"

It was just like him to express aloud the concerns she was trying desperately to silence in her head. "I don't know. But I've gotta try."

He gave a slight nod. She performed a quick internet search on her phone and located the number. How had anyone survived not knowing the well-being of loved ones in pre–cell phone days?

After fifteen minutes of being transferred multiple times and finally getting to talk to someone in the ER, she disconnected. "All they could tell me was that she is stable and the doctor will talk to me once I get to the hospital."

"Stable is good, right?"

"I don't know. It may be their standard reply to anyone who calls to ask about a patient." She bit her lower lip.

"I'm sure she's receiving the best care."

"I know. But what if her attacker gets to her before we can?" Grace shifted in her seat, the vinyl squeaking in protest.

He activated the blinker and took the access ramp onto an almost empty interstate. "I already have a guard outside her door."

"Who? How did you get someone there so fast?" She studied his profile. While some men his age were graying, his copper-colored hair had developed blond highlights, which made him look younger than his thirty-three years.

"Do you remember Ryan Vincent?"

"Played football with you, right? Was two or three years behind us in school? His parents own the Flying V Ranch." She paused, picturing the family that hosted church fellowship picnics on their ranch every summer on the Fourth of July. "He had four brothers and one sister… I don't remember her name…but she and Chloe were good friends in school."

"Yeah. Well, Ryan is now co-owner of the private security agency Protective Instincts, based in Denver. On the drive to the clinic, I called to see if he had a bodyguard he could send to the hospital until we got there."

Relief washed over her. "I'm so glad he could send someone."

"Actually, Ryan is the guard outside Chloe's room. His sister—Bridget—is at the hospital, too. On lookout in the waiting room."

"Really? Wow. Send me their bill when you receive it. I'm more than happy to pay whatever it costs."

He shook his head, a frown marring his face. "You don't get it, do you?" Sadness laced his words. "Ryan and Bridget are helping a friend from home. They aren't going to send a bill requesting payment for the time they're at the hospital tonight."

"But protecting people is their business. Not paying

them would be like going to a doctor who's an acquaintance and expecting a free examination."

"No. It's like being at the park and twisting your ankle. The town doctor who has known you your entire life is there. He wraps your ankle and instructs you to ice it when you get home. He will not send you a bill, unless you go to him for follow-up treatments. Then he'll bill you for his services." Evan spared her a quick glance before turning his attention back to the road. "If we need to hire Protective Instincts to provide around-the-clock protection for Chloe—which is likely, unless I can get the Denver PD to provide a guard—then we'll figure out how they need to bill their services."

Grace opened her mouth and closed it again. Evan would think she had lost her mind if she mentioned she'd rather hire someone who wasn't from Blackberry Falls to guard Chloe, and rightfully so. Grace's fear of others knowing her business and her discomfort with the gossip that went with the small town way of life weren't important right now. Chloe's safety was. Grace would have to withstand the scrutiny that came with others knowing she'd failed to protect her little sister, just as she'd withstood the numerous times her teachers had marched her to her mother's classroom to tell her mother how disobedient she had been.

"Now, what's in the bag?" Evan interrupted her thoughts.

"Chloe's laptop." She pulled the laptop out of the tote sitting beside her feet on the floorboard and settled it on her lap. "I also swiped a couple of hard-copy files from her desk. They were open, so I'm assuming they're files she was working on that kept her at the office so late today. I'll look at those after we get someplace where I can lay everything out. I thought I'd see if I could find clues to help us figure out why someone would want to hurt Chloe." *And me.* Opening the screen, she pressed the power button.

"You think her attack is connected to the clinic?"

"I'm not sure. Last week, she discovered drugs missing from the clinic inventory." Grace drummed her fingers on the laptop as she waited for it to boot up.

"What kind of drugs?"

"Clenbuterol and Levothyroxine."

He frowned.

So she explained, "Clenbuterol is a steroid-like drug used to treat breathing disorders in animals, and Levothyroxine is a synthetic T4 hormone replacement used to treat hypothyroidism in both humans and animals."

"Could those drugs be used to make a horse run faster?"

"It's illegal to do so, but yes." Grace typed in the pass code and the computer desktop filled the screen.

"You know your sister's password?"

"It was a guess."

"Obviously a good one. You got it right the first try."

"Chloe doesn't like change, so I tried the password she used for the laptop Dad bought her for her eleventh birthday." Her smile quivered. The memory of Chloe as a child engulfed her. She had thought she was so grown, getting her very own computer. Grace had felt like her father was spoiling his youngest daughter, but he'd insisted the gift was more about providing his girls with a way to stay in touch once Grace left for college than it was giving Chloe free rein on the internet.

That might have been when Chloe's need to video chat when she was in scary situations first developed. She would call Grace at all hours of the night, so she wouldn't feel alone when Dad had been called out to tend to sick animals. Chloe hadn't been left home alone often, but obviously enough for the seeds of dependency to take root.

The screen blurred. She squeezed her eyes tight, fighting the tears burning for release. *Thank you, Lord, for letting me get to Chloe before he could kill her. I'll never complain about her need to video chat again.*

"She'll be okay." Evan's soft baritone filled the silence.

Grace appreciated his attempt to comfort her, but he couldn't know that any more than she did. She concentrated on her breathing as she tried to think of a response.

"I know they sound like empty words. But I mean it. Chloe's a fighter. Always has been."

"Are we talking about the same girl?" What did he know? When Grace dated him, they'd spent most of their time trying to avoid Chloe with her prying eyes and her constant desire to tag along wherever they went. "Growing up, she never did anything for herself. Always wanting help with her homework and dragging me to the barn to help feed her menagerie of animals."

"That wasn't because she needed help or because she was scared. It was because she loved you and wanted to spend as much time with you as possible. She always knew you'd leave Blackberry Falls."

She sucked in a breath. His words hit like a verbal jab to the heart. His gaze met hers. Breaking contact, she looked down, pretending to focus on the computer screen, tears stinging the backs of her eyes.

Evan cleared his throat. "Other than Chloe's concerns about the clinic, is there anything else going on in her life that might help us determine who's behind the attack?"

"You mean besides her divorce?"

"For the moment, yes."

Ben Hamilton's name came to mind. How did one accuse their father's oldest friend and lifelong neighbor of attempted murder? And for what, a mere eighty acres of land? She rubbed the back of her neck.

"Come on. Out with it. Even if you think it's nothing. We can't afford to overlook any leads."

"Chloe has been receiving letters—offers to buy the farm—from Benjamin Hamilton. He's been getting more persistent lately, even going so far as to tell her why a woman shouldn't live on a farm alone." She sighed. "Looks like he was right. She should have sold to him."

He smiled at her. "Not necessarily. And since we can't change the past, we need to focus on the here and now, which means solving this crime and stopping the attacker from getting to you."

Grace's temples throbbed. *Please don't be a migraine.* She clicked the laptop off, shut the lid and then slipped it into the bag. Leaning back in her seat, she rubbed her tired eyes.

"You didn't find anything useful?"

"I'm not sure what I'm looking for, and my head is starting to hurt." She looked around, trying to figure out where they were. Somewhere along I-25. In the dark, it was hard to tell where exactly. "How much farther?"

"We're almost to the Castle Rock exit. I'd say we're about forty minutes away."

That sounded about right. For the most part, traffic had been light on the drive, but as they got closer to Denver, it would pick up, though 2:00 a.m. traffic wouldn't be anything like the rush hour traffic she'd experienced the evening before. Had it really been less than seven hours since she'd traveled this road in the opposite direction?

"Grace, do you think James could be behind the attack?"

She sat straighter and shifted to look at his profile. "I'm not sure. Before tonight I would have said there was no way. I worried that they'd rushed into marriage. You know, they only dated four months, but from the very beginning, he seemed to dote on her. I first sensed something was wrong at Dad's funeral, but even then, Chloe wouldn't confide in me. It wasn't until…"

He prodded. "Until what?"

Grace had been sworn to secrecy. Did she have the right to share Chloe's secret shame? If James was behind the attack, it could be important to the case. She worried her lower lip.

"Grace. Until what?"

"A year ago, Chloe admitted James had a gambling problem. He'd put them thousands of dollars in debt. She asked me for a loan."

"Did you give it to her?"

"Of course I did. Then a few months ago, right before she filed the divorce paperwork, Chloe confided James had a mistress. Apparently, it wasn't his first."

"Oh, man. It's common knowledge James can be overly friendly to the ladies, but I didn't know he'd cheated on Chloe. Do you know the name of his mistress?"

"I don't remember the name. It was one of the vet techs. Chloe fired her, so she doesn't work at the clinic any longer."

"Marcia O'Neal," Evan stated. "I thought it was odd she took a job at the veterinary hospital in Colorado Springs but continued to live in Blackberry Falls, driving an hour each way to work."

The fact Marcia O'Neal's new job and commute were common knowledge to the chief of police, and most likely ninety percent of the population of Blackberry Falls, didn't shock Grace, but she was thankful at least some of her sister's marital woes had escaped the grapevine.

Hope sparked in her. "If James is behind the attack, why would I be a target? Do you think it was an empty threat to throw us off the trail?"

"Um, I don't think so. For starters, you saw the attacker's face…" He glanced in the rearview mirror and increased his speed. "And it seems we picked up a tail around the Castle Rock exit."

Grace looked out the rear window, the headlights of a vehicle gaining on them temporarily blinding her. Turning back around, she blinked several times to regain focus. "If they've been following us for ten miles, why didn't you try to lose them sooner?"

"I wasn't sure the truck was following us until a couple of miles back. When I sped up and passed those two 18-wheelers, it made every move I did."

"What do we do? We can't lead them to Chloe."

"I don't think getting to Chloe is their priority right now."

"Why do you say that?" She heard the panic in her own voice.

"Because they're making their presence well-known, staying almost bumper-to-bumper."

As if to punctuate his words, the full-size pickup rammed them from behind. Evan jerked the steering wheel to the right and took the exit ramp off the interstate.

The pickup shadowed their every move.

"Grace, get down!"

The authority in his voice had her sliding to the floor as a bullet hit the rear window of their SUV, passed through her headrest and embedded itself in the dashboard.

The threat hadn't been a ruse.

Someone wanted her dead.

* * *

Evan had no clue where they were, but estimated Denver city limits was approximately twenty miles away. He hated being in unfamiliar surroundings. His only hope was to lose the vehicle in one of the many suburban neighborhoods and get back on the interstate as soon as possible.

"Are you going to be able to lose him?"

"I'll do my best." The light ahead turned yellow. He gunned the motor. "Hang on." He sped into the intersection—thankful it was the middle of the night and there were no other vehicles around—and, at the last second, turned the wheel sharply to the left, barely missing a light pole. The driver of the truck shot through the intersection.

"Whew. You did it!" Grace's relief exhilarated him, but only momentarily because he knew the driver would maneuver a U-turn and be back on their tail.

"I only bought us a little time. I'm sure he's turning around as we speak." He scanned the area as they sped past a drugstore, gas station and small city park. Did he dare try to find a place to park in the hope the driver wouldn't find them? There didn't seem to be any place to hide, no other vehicles to blend in with. No. Keep moving.

He turned right. Being in unfamiliar surroundings was like being a blindfolded mouse in a maze. He took a left turn and found himself in a neighborhood behind the park.

Evan felt vulnerable. The area was too open. He looked at Grace. Her eyes were closed, her head bowed as if in prayer. She was as innocent as she'd always been. Let her hold to her faith, he'd trust in his own abilities. Flipping the switch on the end of the turn signal lever, he turned off his lights and inched along the sleepy neighborhood street. Headlights swept across the park.

Guided only by the sliver of moonlight, he pulled to the curb and parked in-line with the other cars in front of a row of houses and waited for their pursuer to speed past the park. But the driver didn't speed past. Instead, he turned onto the very street where they waited.

No way to hide a Blackberry Falls police SUV in a Denver suburb. Evan bit back an exclamation, flicked on the lights and raced down the street as fast as he dared.

"He found us." Grace's voice was barely above a whisper.

"Yeah. But don't count me out yet." Evan tried to sound reassuring, but he could hear the doubt in his voice. Why hadn't he changed vehicles? Driving this one was like flashing a neon sign telling the attacker where to find Grace.

He made several turns, barely staying ahead of the other driver who'd backed off enough to allow himself time to follow Evan's movements. No shots this time. Their pursuer was probably afraid of the prying eyes of a Neighborhood Watch member.

Grace dug into her purse and pulled out her phone. "Shouldn't we call nine-one-one?"

"Only if I can't lose him. In the meantime, use your phone to pinpoint our location. Just in case."

Relaying their exact location would be hard. With his lack of knowledge of the area, Evan couldn't give street names or landmarks to guide the police. His best hope was that an officer cruising the night streets would come upon them speeding through town.

He turned toward what he assumed was the main street and came to an immediate halt. A mechanical railroad-crossing arm blocked his path. The freight engine's light pierced the night, its horn echoing in the silence.

"What are we going to do?" Grace's panicked voice was barely audible above the train's horn.

Their tormentor loomed behind them. They were easy targets for his bullets now. The truck reversed. The hair on the back of Evan's neck prickled. The driver intended to make their deaths look like an accident.

"Hang on to something. He's going to hit us." Evan engaged the emergency brake and pressed firmly on the floor brake while turning the steering wheel to the right. The SUV jolted, tires squealing and smoke billowing in through the air vents. The breaks held, the impact only moving them a few inches forward. The driver of the truck reversed again. He was building up speed.

Evan released the emergency brake and turned the wheel even more sharply to the right, toward the service road that ran parallel to the tracks. If his plan worked, their attacker might crash, but he and Grace would escape without injury.

"One… Two…" He counted, trying to time their escape. "Three." He jerked the wheel and pressed the gas pedal to the floor when the truck was inches from hitting them. They flew along the service road, and he watched in his rearview mirror as the pickup did a donut spin and come to a stop pointed in the opposite direction. The driver had escaped the collision. It would be a matter of seconds before he started chasing them again. There was only one option.

Picking up speed, Evan raced the train to the next intersection.

"You're going to try to outrun the train!" Horror tainted Grace's accusation. He knew she was thinking about eleventh grade when Tommy Smithfield tried to cross in front of a train one time too many.

"It's our only option." He didn't dare spare a glance in her direction. "I'll only cut in front of it if I know without a doubt I can make it. I promise." *Please, Lord, help me keep Grace safe.* The prayer came unbidden. Would God answer Evan when he hadn't spoken to Him in so long?

Evan's SUV was neck and neck with the train's engine at the first intersection. He'd have to try the next one. The pursuing lights in his rearview mirror were gaining on them. The next intersection loomed ahead. Warning lights flashed and the mechanical arm started its descent. Evan pressed harder on the gas pedal, shooting forward. *Thank you, Lord.* They would make it.

"Hang on," he ordered Grace for what seemed like the umpteenth time.

Grace's scream mingled with the freight train's horn.

Evan's heart jackhammered against his rib cage as they bounced across the tracks mere seconds ahead of the locomotive. He exhaled. They'd survived. The driver of the truck had been trapped on the other side of the tracks.

Grace was curled into as tight of a ball as possible with her knees pulled to her chest, arms wrapped tightly around them and her head tucked. Her scream turned to sobs. He reached across and touched her arm. "It's okay. We're okay."

Evan's throat tightened as guilt assailed him. If he had changed vehicles, or taken a different route, or something, maybe he could have avoided putting her through this additional trauma. He slid his hand down her arm and laced his fingers with hers, trying to offer calming comfort as his thumb caressed the back of her hand.

He pushed the voice command button on the steering

wheel and asked for directions to Denver Memorial that would avoid the interstate.

Several minutes later, Grace's sobs quieted, and she took several deep, concentrated breaths. She pulled her hand free. "I'm sorry. I didn't mean to lose it."

"You've had a traumatic evening."

"Yes, but I should have trusted you. I know you don't take unnecessary chances." She straightened, the seat squeaking with her movement, and peered at the clock on the dashboard: 2:36 a.m. They should have been at the hospital long ago. The cat and mouse game with the man who wanted her and Chloe dead had cost them half an hour.

"How much farther?"

"We should be there in about ten minutes." He nodded toward the map displayed on the screen mounted above the radio. "Sorry, but I thought it best to stay off the interstate. It's less likely our *friend* will find us this way."

"How did you program the map while…" Her words faltered.

Holding her hand?

"Voice command." As if to qualify what he'd said, an animated voice directed him to turn at the next light.

"What if the guy in the truck beats us to the hospital?"

"I think we have a good chance of getting there and out of sight before him. I've been going well above the speed limit to stay ahead of him. Also, with as many hospitals as there are in the Denver metro area, unless he knows exactly which hospital Chloe was taken to, it's likely he'll end up at one of the other ones. No matter what, we'll be on guard."

His cell phone rang, and he pushed the hands-free button on the steering wheel. "Bradshaw here."

"Evan, this is Ryan. You're behind schedule. Is everything okay?"

"We ran into a little trouble. But we're okay. Only a few blocks away. Tell Bridget to watch for us." He disconnected the call.

The automated GPS voice directed him to turn right and take the second left, where they would reach their destination.

He pulled into the ER drop-off area, and Grace unfastened her seat belt, ready to bolt through the doors as soon as he stopped.

"Do not open your door."

"But—"

"Bridget will meet us at the entrance. I'll escort you inside, and she'll park the vehicle."

Letting a civilian drive his police vehicle broke all kinds of rules and regulations, but at this point Evan wasn't ready to trust Grace's safety to anyone other than himself.

FOUR

Every muscle in Grace's body was on high alert, and she desperately wanted to spring out of the vehicle. It had been over three and a half hours since she'd watched the medics put her unresponsive sister into a med-flight helicopter. Much longer and she wouldn't be able to suppress the frustrated scream that clawed at her throat begging for release.

"I need a moment to assess the area and make sure we're safe. Stay seated until I come around." Evan slammed the vehicle into Park and bolted from the driver's seat. He had barely stepped out of the SUV when a petite woman with short, pixie-cut, auburn hair slid into his recently vacated spot.

"Hi, Grace. I don't know if you remember me. Bridget Vincent. Ryan—my brother—is inside guarding Chloe." Bridget prattled on saying something about getting the call from Evan and rushing to the hospital, but Grace couldn't comprehend her words.

She stared at the miniature ball of energy. Bridget had grown into a beautiful woman, but she still talked at warp speed, as if it were some kind of race to see who could get out the most words between breaths.

"Uh…yeah… I remember you," Grace managed to say when Bridget paused.

"We're praying for Chloe. She's a fighter. I'm sure she'll pull through—"

The passenger door opened. "Thanks, Bridget," Evan said as his hand cupped Grace's elbow, helping her out of the SUV. "Don't forget to lock the doors and bring me the keys."

"Sure. No problem. You know I don't mind at—"

Evan closed the door, cutting off Bridget's words, and strode toward the ER entrance, Grace almost sprinting as she struggled to match his pace. "Wasn't trying to be rude, but man, that woman can talk the ears off a donkey."

"That's not nice."

His eyes shone with amusement, and she giggled in spite of herself. Their laughter mingled, echoing off the concrete walls. For a moment, tension lifted from her shoulders and her chest felt less constricted, her breathing lighter. Then guilt assaulted her. How could she laugh with her sister in the hospital fighting for her life?

Evan squeezed her hand and guided her to the security checkpoint. He flashed his badge and explained the situation to the guard. Once they had passes, a nurse escorted them past the main waiting area, through a maze of hallways and into what Grace assumed was the trauma section of the ER.

A man with short black hair, wearing square-framed, black-rimmed glasses, sat in a chair outside Room 13A. Ryan? Bridget had been easily recognizable, but Grace would not have recognized Ryan. It wasn't that his appearance had changed much, but more that he had an air of seriousness and no-nonsense.

How he had gotten permission to stay in this area and

guard her sister's door, Grace may never know, but she would be eternally grateful. He stood, shook Evan's hand and then gave her a hug like she was a cousin he hadn't seen in a while.

"I'm sorry this happened." He pulled back and looked her in the eyes, his hands on her shoulders. "But she's in the best place for the best care. We haven't worked out all the details yet, but Bridget and I will help coordinate around-the-clock guard protection until they catch her attacker."

Words failed her, so Grace simply nodded.

A tall, silver-haired, tanned gentleman wearing scrubs and a white lab coat came out of Chloe's room.

"Grace, this is Dr. Carson." Ryan made introductions. "Sir, this is Chloe's sister, Dr. Grace Porter. And Police Chief Evan Bradshaw."

"Dr. Porter."

"DVM not MD." She hurriedly shook the offered hand. "How's my sister? Is she awake?"

"No. Not yet." Dr. Carson moved aside and motioned for her to enter the room ahead of him. "Let's step inside."

She looked to Evan. Would he come with her?

"I need to talk to Ryan. I'll be in soon."

Grace nodded, took a deep breath and went into the room where heart rate monitors and numerous other machines beeped and flashed. Chloe had been intubated, a breathing tube down her throat. She lay perfectly still. Her skin was pasty and there was an ugly bluish-purple bruise on the side of her face. At least she didn't appear to be in distress.

"Is she in pain?" Grace whispered.

"No." Dr. Carson walked over to the monitors and checked the readings before turning back to face her.

"We've placed your sister in a medically induced coma. She suffered a brain hemorrhage."

Grace gasped, and he rushed on. "There's a good deal of swelling because of inflammation from the broken vessels, but all scans indicate the bleeding has stopped. Other than that, she has three cracked ribs and a broken wrist. All in all, I'd say Chloe is a very fortunate lady."

"Fortunate? She almost died, and now she's in a coma." The smell of antiseptic mingled with the sharp, stabbing pain behind Grace's left eye, and her vision blurred. This migraine was gearing up to be a doozy. She gripped the bed rail as she fought nausea.

"Medically induced. Once the swelling goes down, we'll wake her up." The doctor touched Grace's arm and searched her face. "Dr. Porter, are you sick?"

"A headache." She puffed out a breath and forced a smile. "I'll be fine. Once I'm sure Chloe's okay. Will she make a full recovery?"

"I can't guarantee anything, but if all goes as planned, then yes."

"And if it doesn't?" Grace questioned, not wanting the answer but needing to know. Bile burning the back of her throat, she rode the wave of pain assailing her.

The doctor hesitated, and she met his gaze. "Please, I need to know."

He gave a nod of agreement. "If the swelling continues, we'll do surgery to relieve the pressure, but she could suffer permanent brain damage."

"And that would mean?"

"At the very least, problems with her fine motor skills and her speech."

Please, Lord, don't let him say it.

"Worst case scenario, she would be in a vegetative state. But I will do everything in my power to keep that from happening." He pulled a chair up closer to the bed, and she sank into it. "Be sure to take something for that headache. I need to go see how much longer it will be until we have a bed for Chloe in the Neuro ICU. You can stay with her until she's moved."

She gasped. "Dr. Carson, the person who attacked my sister is still on the loose. I know ICU staff monitors patients closely, but she can't be unattended at any time."

He squeezed her shoulder. "Don't worry. I'm not sure how he did it, but the young bodyguard out there secured permission from the chief of staff to have a guard stationed outside her room at all times, even in the ICU."

He pulled a peppermint out of his coat pocket and dropped it into her hand. "Maybe this will help until you can eat and take some meds." Dr. Carson gave her a grandfatherly smile and walked out of the room.

Grace scooted closer to Chloe's bed and wrapped her hand around her sister's cold one. "Oh, Chloe. Please wake up soon and tell us who did this to you. I don't know who I can trust—other than Evan—and I can't keep leaning on him. It would be too easy to fall into old habits, and that wouldn't be good for either of us. He thrives in small town America. You know me, Chloe. Have I ever enjoyed living where I have to wonder who's gossiping about me? Nope." She caressed her sister's hand, wishing she could laugh with her. "You remember the time—"

A creak sounded behind her, and she whirled around. How long had Evan been there? What had he heard?

Evan paced the length of the waiting area and back again. Bits and pieces of Grace's one-sided conversation with Chloe tumbled around in his brain. Why did she always have to see their hometown through such a narrow lens?

His phone vibrated. Lieutenant Johnson's name flashed on the screen.

"Bradshaw here." He spoke in a hushed tone.

"Chief, I wanted to let you know we finished interviewing Dr. James Osborne."

"And?"

"At the time of the attack, he was eating dinner at Aunt Bea's Diner on Highway 9. The owner has been very cooperative and shared the video footage. Osborne arrived at 8:17 p.m. Sat in a booth at the back of the restaurant. Approximately ten minutes later, a brunette in her early- to mid-twenties joined him. She looked familiar, but I've not been able to ID her yet. And Osborne is refusing to give her name."

"Marcia O'Neal."

"Sir?"

"There's a very good chance the woman is a vet tech that the doctor was seeing on the side. Her name is Marcia O'Neal."

"I'll try to verify that information. But, sir, this means his alibi checks out."

"I'm not surprised. Grace saw the attacker's face, so we know it wasn't him. Doesn't mean he isn't behind the attack, though."

"Agreed."

"What do your instincts tell you?" A body language expert, Johnson had an uncanny ability to read people, and Evan trusted his instincts.

"Dr. Osborne seemed genuinely upset about the attack."

"But?"

"I couldn't get a clear sense of his guilt or innocence. He's hiding something. If he's not behind the attack, I suspect he has a good idea who is."

As small as his police force was, Evan didn't have the manpower to assign officers to watch James Osborne 24/7. He loved being the police chief in a small town, but there were drawbacks, especially when it came to funding. "Okay. Fill the other officers in on what we know so far and make sure they 'unofficially' keep track of the doctor's whereabouts."

"Will do. Anything else?" the lieutenant asked.

"Hold down the fort until I get back."

"When will that be?"

A soft snore pulled his attention back to the room.

Grace had fallen asleep, twisted sideways in a lime-green, vinyl chair, her legs draped across the arm and her head tilted awkwardly against the wall. He knew exhaustion had claimed her soon after her sister had been moved to a room in Neuro ICU. Earlier, she'd downed two pain pills and guzzled a vending machine coffee. He hoped her headache was gone when she woke but was afraid it would be replaced with a crick in her neck. Sitting beside Grace, Bridget flipped through a magazine, lifting her gaze to the door every few seconds, always on alert.

"Chief? Are you still there?" Johnson's voice sounded in his ear.

"Yeah. My goal is to be back by three so I can pick Camden up from school." He looked out the bank of windows on the east-facing wall of the waiting room. The sun had risen, and traffic was increasing. The morning rush hour would soon be in full swing. "I still need to finalize a plan to provide around-the-clock guards for Chloe."

"About that. The patrol officers and I have decided we'll take care of guard duty."

"I wish it were that easy." Evan sighed. "Not only can I not afford to pay overtime for you guys to serve as guards, but it's over a two-hour drive, one-way."

"No, you don't understand. We're volunteering our time on our days off."

"What? Are you serious? I can't ask you to do that."

"You're not asking."

"But—"

"No, sir." Johnson cut him off. "We've made our minds up. Chloe Osborne is one of our own. Most of us have known her since grade school. A few of us even took her out a time or two in high school, myself included. Blackberry Falls is about community and family. We take care of both."

Can't argue with his logic.

To be honest, Evan was relieved he wouldn't have to approach the Denver chief to ask for assistance. They'd had words the night Lisa had been killed in a drive-by shooting a block from the hotel where they were staying. Granted, Evan bore most of the responsibility for agreeing to walk back to the hotel following the play instead of insisting on taking a cab. He had known the streets could be dangerous at that time of night, but Lisa had wanted to enjoy the evening a little longer. The hotel had been less than two blocks away, and she could be very persuasive when she wanted to be. He'd been happy to see her smile again.

"All right, then. Text me a schedule of the rotation. I'll pass it along to Ryan, so he can notify the hospital staff. He and Bridget will also fill in any gaps in the schedule as needed. Oh—and, Johnson, make sure the officers know if their relief is late arriving, they are not to leave their post, even if it means they're late for work. We'll cover for them, and their pay won't be docked."

"Yes, sir."

Disconnecting the call, Evan slipped the phone into his pocket. An elderly man with a walker entered the waiting area, followed by a blue-haired woman of similar age and a dark-haired girl who looked to be in her early twenties. The hospital buzzed with morning activity. As much as he'd like to let Grace sleep a little longer, he needed to wake her and find a more private area for them to discuss a plan to keep her safe after he headed home.

Home. Growing up moving from one military base to the other, Blackberry Falls had felt like home from the moment his family had settled there following his father's retirement from the Air Force. The moment he'd first seen the town—its Main Street decorated with American flags for Memorial Day, the large park at the center of the town square, and the endless hiking trails into the Rocky Mountains with one leading to the waterfall the town had been named for—he had known he never wanted to leave.

Just one of the reasons he would never understand why Grace had been in such a hurry to leave the only home she'd ever known.

Grace's migraine had lessened, but her senses remained on hyper alert—even the roots of her hair ached. She rubbed her temples and tried to focus on Evan's words.

"I've worked everything out. You can be in the comfort of your own home and be here for your sister. Bridget will stay with you at night and bring you back to the hospital each morning."

He wanted her to stay in Denver? She had felt certain he'd insist on her returning to Blackberry Falls where he could keep an eye on her.

"One of my off-duty officers will be here, stationed right outside Chloe's door." Evan looked at her, then continued in a rush. "You'll have to stay in Chloe's room, only stepping out and staying with the guard when the doctors or nurses ask you to. At the end of the day, Ryan or Bridget will pick you up and escort you home. No venturing out, because I won't have a guard who can go with you. Do you understand?"

Relief flooded through her. She'd stay by her sister's bedside and watch over her, ensuring her safety. Then a niggle of doubt worked its way into her brain. The doctors and nurses were the people her sister needed to take care of her, not Grace. They were the ones who could make her comfortable. And the off-duty police officers who—for whatever reason she could not imagine—were volunteering time away from their own families, were the ones who could protect her. There wasn't much Grace could do here.

She bit her lower lip. Staying at the hospital would be selfish. Grace would be hiding out. She'd be a bigger help to her sister if she went back to Blackberry Falls, took care of the clinic and looked for clues as to who wanted them both dead. "No. I mean yes, I understand. No, I won't stay here."

"Don't be stubborn, Gracie." Evan dragged a hand over his face where stubble had transformed his normally clean-cut, guy-next-door look into one of a rugged outdoorsman. "I knew you wouldn't enjoy having to stay in one place all day, but it's the best I can do."

"It's not that. I need to take care of things at the clinic."

If she couldn't make him understand, he'd insist she stay here, under lock and key. "James is scheduled to leave at the end of next week, after they finalize the divorce. In the meantime, I need him to go over the patient files with me and fill me in on the ins and outs of his caseload. I also need to start interviewing for a new vet. Besides, I also have Barkley to consider. He'll be sad his owner is missing and will need extra attention."

"Be reasonable." His voice boomed in the small walk-in-closet-size room where they waited to talk with Dr. Carson and receive an update on Chloe. Lowering his voice, Evan added, "I don't have the manpower to protect you at the clinic."

"I'll be fine at the clinic. I won't be alone. There are always a lot of people around."

"What about after work? Who will guard you then? Am I going to have to spend the nights in my car outside the farmhouse waiting for the man to come back to try to kill you?"

"No. You have a child who needs you at home. Look. I know you'd prefer to keep me under twenty-four-hour security, miles away from Blackberry Falls, but do you think that will stop someone who wants me dead?"

He paled, as if she'd slapped him. She'd heard he'd been walking right beside his wife when she was shot and hadn't been able to stop it from happening. Knowing him as well as she did, she knew he blamed himself. He needn't worry. Grace had lived on her own for almost half her life. She knew how to be cautious and wouldn't take unnecessary risks.

"I'll stay in the apartment above the clinic. It's only a few miles from the police station, and I'll set the alarm system the second the last employee leaves."

"What if the last employee to leave is James? We've not ruled him out as a suspect yet."

"I'll make sure he isn't the last one."

"How can you guarantee that?"

"I'll come up with some excuse for him to leave early, an errand or something. If that fails, I'll leave with the other employees. I'm sure Valerie would be happy to drive me to the police station."

Valerie had been an employee at the clinic longer than anyone else, starting as a part-time employee in high school and later becoming a veterinary technician. She had become a close family friend. Grace knew she'd do as asked without question.

"Once you get off work, you can take me back to the clinic, check everything out, and make sure things are locked up tight."

Evan still looked doubtful, so she added, "I promise to be careful, but if these attacks are connected to whatever Chloe discovered at the clinic, you'll need someone on the inside looking for clues."

"I think you've been watching too many whodunit movies."

"No, but I enjoy true crime shows. Do you have enough info to secure a search warrant at the clinic?"

"No. However, as co-owner, you can give us permission without a warrant."

"I can give you access to general information, like billing and drug supplies, not patient records. That would be unethical. If you found something in the records I gave you access to, James would probably be long gone before you could secure a search warrant for his files. Admit it, you need my help."

He shoved his hand through his hair. "If I go along with this, you must promise not to take any risks. I have to know your whereabouts at all times."

She'd never liked having her every move analyzed, but if that's what it took to get him to let her go back to help look for the person wanting her and Chloe dead, then so be it.

FIVE

Evan was late. He turned onto the road that circled around to the back of Blackberry Falls Elementary School and pulled into the car-rider pickup line, nodding a return greeting to parents who waved as they drove past. There were a dozen or so cars ahead of him in line. Hopefully, Camden hadn't become apprehensive. The anxiety attacks had started the second month of kindergarten, when Evan had been late because he'd stopped to offer aid to a stranded motorist. The counselor had told him the attacks were a result of Camden's fear of something happening to his only living parent.

Camden had only been twenty months old when Lisa died, too young to have many memories of her. When he'd started school and had realized most of his classmates had two parents, he'd started crying himself to sleep at night and didn't want to let Evan out of his sight.

The car in front of them pulled forward, and he followed. Only five cars ahead of him now, he was close enough to see the children waiting on the sidewalk, their backs against the building. Camden stood next to the assistant principal, Ms. Sims, his gaze downcast and shoulders slouched.

His son's pain ripped at Evan's heart, which was why

he'd do anything within his power to eliminate his fears, including dragging Grace to the school. "I'm sorry I wasn't able to drop you off at the clinic first. It's important for me to pick Camden up on time."

She nodded. "It's fine."

"Lisa's mom normally picks Cam up, but she and her husband had to fly to Arizona for the birth of a grandchild. They'll be gone for two weeks." Which was why Cam had spent the night with them last night, a school night, and why Evan had been the one to respond to Grace's 9-1-1 call.

"It's okay, I understand."

"Thank you. Did you get a chance to talk to Valerie?" He still wasn't convinced Grace's plan was a good one. However, he also couldn't guarantee any of the clinic employees were safe, with or without her presence. For the time being, he'd increase the patrols in the area, and he'd make a point of either him or another officer being at the clinic before the end of day. They could help her lock up and secure the premises.

"No. Other than a text early this morning asking her to take care of Barkley until I got back. I can fill her in once we get to the clinic."

"Don't tell her too much. The fewer people who know we suspect a connection to the clinic, the better."

"Don't worry. I'm not one who overshares."

Evan remembered. Like she hadn't shared her intentions of going away to school and never returning.

He pulled forward. Ms. Sims said something to Camden, and he looked up and spotted the police vehicle, relief flooding his little face. Evan waved.

The car in front of them pulled away from the curb, and he slid into the vacated spot, rolling down the window. "Sorry I'm late."

"It's okay, Dad." The words sounded good, but the smile looked forced. Poor guy. Evan had called his mom earlier to see if she could pick Camden up, but she'd been at a dentist's appointment. There were less than two weeks left in the school year, but next year, Evan would need a better backup plan for someone to pick up Camden from school in an emergency.

"You're not late at all, chief." The administrator opened the back door, and Camden climbed into the booster seat Evan had hurriedly picked up at a big-box store on their return from Denver. "See you, Monday, Camden." Mrs. Sims shut the door and waved Evan on, ensuring the car-rider line ran like a well-oiled machine.

He pulled up to the stop sign and glanced in his rearview mirror. "Hey, sport. Did you have a good day?" Camden didn't reply. His gaze was fixed on Grace. "Camden, this is Dr. Porter. She's a veterinarian. We're giving her a ride to Porter Animal Clinic."

The smile that split Cam's face was genuine and reached all the way to the green eyes he'd inherited from his mother. "Oh, boy! Can I pet the animals?"

"It's not a zoo—"

"You can't pet the patients," Grace interrupted, twisting in her seat to smile at Camden. "But I'm sure Barkley would love some attention."

"Gracie, I'm—"

"Who's Barkley?" Camden asked.

"My sister's dog. I'm dog-sitting him for a while."

"Is he a puppy?"

She giggled. "No, he's a full-grown dog."

"Full-grown pony," Evan muttered under his breath. In his peripheral vision, he saw Grace's smile widen. She'd heard him.

A horn blared behind them. Great. He'd stalled the

movement of the car-rider line. He pulled out of the parking lot and headed north, half listening to the conversation between Grace and his son.

"How old is Barkley?"

"He's three."

"Three?" Shock laced Camden's little voice. "He's a baby. I'm six. I'm more grown than him," he added emphatically.

Don't rush it son. Don't rush it.

A melodious laugh emanated from Grace. "I don't think anyone can call Barkley a baby. Wait until you meet him. He's bigger than you are."

"No way," Camden protested. Then he started telling Grace all the things he was taller than.

A grin tugged at Evan's lips. When he'd seen Camden's crestfallen face, he'd been sure it would be a long, quiet ride home, but somehow Grace had turned it around.

Ten minutes later, he pulled the SUV into the parking lot of the Porter Animal Clinic. The lot was empty, except for the two vehicles in the employee parking area at the side of the building. One was James Osborne's luxury sports car, but Evan wasn't sure who owned the other, less pretentious, economy vehicle.

"Looks like business is slow today," he said, parking in the spot closest to the front door.

"What? That doesn't make sense. I imagined the place would be swamped with nosy busybodies wanting to get the latest gossip."

"Grace, the people in this town care about your sister. If they're talking about her, it's not to gossip. It's because they're worried."

"Wait. There's a sign on the door," Grace noted, ignoring his words. She leaned forward. "'Temporarily closed because of a family emergency.'"

She unfastened her seat belt and opened her door. "What are they thinking?"

"Hold on." Evan bolted out of his seat and rushed around the back of the vehicle, scanning the area. Nothing seemed out of place.

"Don't forget me, Dad." Camden banged his hand on the window, child security locks preventing him from letting himself out. Evan mentally kicked himself. Why hadn't he found a babysitter for Cam? Because he hadn't known whom to call, since he'd never needed a sitter before with both his and Lisa's parents living close by and happy to help.

Grace had already barged through the door of the clinic. He had to follow her. What about Camden? Would he be safer in the vehicle? The temperatures were still cool, but Evan couldn't take a chance. Nothing to do but let Camden out of the backseat and follow her.

"Son, I need you to obey me at all times while we're here. Do you understand?"

"Yes, sir."

"I mean it, Cam. Don't wander off. Stay where I tell you and listen to all my commands."

"Got it. Now can I see Barkley?"

He escorted his small son into what should have been a fun and exciting environment, but for today was scary and unknown.

Lord, I pray I'm not putting Cam in danger.

Two prayers in one day. Could he be learning to talk to the Lord again?

The twenty-third Psalm instantly sprang to mind.

Grace seethed. What had James been thinking? Why had he closed the clinic today? Dad had never closed the clinic during regular business hours. If he'd been unable to work, the office staff, vet techs and veterinary assistants still reported to the clinic to handle nonmedical emergency issues and to redirect emergencies to a veterinarian in a nearby town.

The waiting area was empty. She glanced in the exam rooms, also empty. Next was James's private office. Again empty. Where was he? She'd seen his vehicle. She knew he was there. The sound of drawers slamming came from her sister's office.

She rounded the receptionist's desk. "James? Why is the clinic closed?"

He strolled out of Chloe's office. "Because I didn't want to spend the day answering questions about why I was here and not at the hospital with Chloe."

"If you didn't want people gossiping about your marital affairs, you should have been faithful to your wife."

James startled, and his eyes widened.

"Yes. Chloe told me. What I'm more interested in right now is what you were doing in her office."

"I don't owe you an explanation." He pushed past her, headed for the front door.

"Actually, you do."

He pivoted on his heel and glared at her. "Do what?"

"Owe me an explanation." She met his eyes and willed her voice to remain steady, while her insides rattled as if an 8.0 quake had shaken the earth. Maybe it was having her life threatened twice in a matter of hours. Maybe it was because she'd failed Chloe as a big sister and she needed to make it right. Normally, Grace hated conflict, but she needed answers. "In case you've forgotten because of my absence, I'm co-owner of the clinic. So that makes me your boss."

He leaned in close. "What are you going to do, fire me? Chloe's lawyer took care of that when he served me with papers. Didn't he? That's why you're here, after all. Well, it's all yours. If you can hold on to it, that is."

The bell over the front door jingled and Evan entered, a firm grasp on Camden's hand.

"Where are the puppy dogs?" Camden struggled to pull free of his dad's grip, but Evan held firm. "Dr. Porter said I could meet Barkley."

"In a minute, son." He escorted the child across the waiting area and stood beside her, his gaze fixed on James. "After Dr. Porter finishes talking to Dr. Osborne."

"We're finished. Dr. Porter was just showing me the door," James scoffed. "Good luck finding someone to replace me." He turned and strode out of the building.

"What was that all about?"

"I'm not sure. He was in Chloe's office. I think he was searching for something." She inhaled sharply. "The tote bag is still in your car. Do you think he was looking for her computer?"

"I don't know." Evan knelt to eye level with his son, the child a miniature version of his father, save for the green eyes. "Stay with Dr. Porter while I get her bag out of the car."

Grace desperately wanted to rush into her sister's office and start searching through files, but she couldn't very well do that with a child in tow. "So, how about we go find Barkley, and then you can help me feed him?"

"Oh, boy!" Camden put his small hand into hers. "I begged Dad for a puppy, but he said I'm not old enough. Dr. Porter, how old do ya have to be to get a pet? My dad's really old! Shouldn't he be old enough to have one? If it was his pet, I could still play with it." The child rattled on while they walked, not pausing long enough for her to respond.

Grace led him toward the rear door. Hopefully, Valerie had put Barkley in the fenced-in kennel area instead of leaving him in the apartment all day. She reached for the knob, but the door opened before she could touch it. She gasped and shoved Camden behind her, blocking him from danger.

"Grace!"

"Oh!" She pressed a hand against her chest, as if the pressure could slow down the hammering of her heart. "Valerie, you startled me."

The tall, slender, black-haired woman who looked like she should be on a runway in New York City stepped across the threshold, Barkley at her heels. "I'm sorry. I was feeding the animals when I saw the chief's SUV pull in. I thought you might be here to pick up Barkley."

The massive Great Dane almost knocked Grace down as he scrambled to check out the little boy peeking from behind her legs. "Camden, this is Barkley."

"He's a giant!" The child stared in awe.

"A gentle giant." She laughed. "Barkley, sit."

The animal obeyed, his tail tapping a steady beat against the concrete floor. Grace knelt and ran her hands through his soft fur, rubbing the back of his neck. "It's okay to pet him. Gently rub your hand over his shoulder. Good."

Barkley licked Camden's face, and the child giggled. "He likes me."

"Of course he does." She stood and faced Valerie. "Thank you for taking care of him today."

"No problem." The veterinarian technician's face grew solemn. "How's Chloe? I heard you saved her—and you saw the attacker's face." Valerie moved in closer and added in a hushed tone, "Can you identify him?"

A shiver went up Grace's arm. How did Valerie know she'd seen the attacker's face? Grace had only told Evan, and he wouldn't have told anyone other than on a need-to-know basis. Her throat constricted. She shook her head and stepped back.

Valerie offered her a sympathetic smile. "I couldn't believe something like that could happen in our small town. Everyone's on edge, wondering if this person will attack again. My mom is even locking her doors in the daytime. Why, I stopped by for lunch today and had to ring the doorbell."

An internal struggle, so familiar in her childhood, started in the pit of Grace's stomach. Be honest with her lifelong friend and admit her fears Chloe wouldn't survive and risk everything she said being front-page news tomorrow, or act as if everything was fine?

"There's no evidence the citizens of Blackberry Falls are in danger." Evan stepped into the hallway and ruffled his son's hair, a smile lighting his face. "But it's always a good idea to keep your doors locked, even in a small town."

Gratitude washed over Grace. Once again, Evan had saved her. He'd done that numerous times in the last nineteen hours. First, protecting her from the person who wanted her dead, and now saving her from answering a difficult question. After fifteen years of being independent and on her own, Grace was afraid she was getting used to him being there for her. And that terrified her.

Grace opened one eye and looked at the clock on the bedside table. Three seventeen. Living alone had never spooked her, and the mental and physical exhaustion of the previous twenty-four hours had given her the hope of a sound night's sleep. Instead, she'd heard every creak and rumble of the night—cars, animals and unidentified thuds and bumps. It had been after midnight before she had closed her eyes, only to awaken every twenty minutes or so. In total, she'd probably slept less than an hour.

She flopped onto her back and stared at the ceiling.

Evan had called a locksmith to change all the locks and codes on every exterior door in the clinic and the apartment. Then he'd insisted on staying with her until Camden's bedtime. He ordered a pizza and chocolate-chip cookies from a local restaurant. After dinner, Camden and Barkley played together on the floor while she and Evan sat on the couch viewing the files on Chloe's computer. To an observer, she was sure the scene would have looked like a typical family evening. That is until Evan checked all the doors, both in the clinic and the apartment, to ensure they were locked, did a full perimeter check, ordered hourly police patrols and drove off into the night with his son, while she and Barkley watched from the window.

Throwing the cover off, Grace got out of bed and plodded into the kitchen for a drink of water. Her mind replayed the events of the day. Why had James been so evasive when Grace had asked what he'd been doing in Chloe's office? He had to have been searching for something. But what?

Her eyes fell upon the tote lying on the small kitchen table, the computer sitting off to the side. She picked up the bag and peered inside. She'd completely forgotten about the file folders. Grace had looked over them briefly at the hospital, but nothing had seemed out of place. What was she missing?

Pulling the files out of the bag, she laid them open. Typical billing records. Dates and types of service, insurance payment, if any, and account balances.

Wait a minute.

She picked up the last folder she had slipped into the

bag, the one that had been half hidden under the desk blotter. These weren't accounting records, they were medical records.

Why would Chloe—who had a master's in business administration and worked as the office manager—have medical records hidden in her office? And why a printed copy? The clinic used an online database to store and streamline patient records. They didn't keep hard-copy files any longer.

She scanned the pages. A toxicology report and a necropsy report. The patient, a three-year-old Thoroughbred stallion named Mountain Shadow, had died of sudden heart failure. At the time of death, in addition to high doses of caffeine, he also had high levels of Clenbuterol and Levothyroxine in his system. The two drugs Chloe had said were missing from inventory.

Grace powered up the computer, then turned and searched the cabinets for coffee pods. She needed something stronger than water since it looked like she wouldn't be going back to bed anytime soon.

Steaming mug in hand, she scooped the laptop off the table and made her way to the faded green-plaid sofa in the small sitting area. Placing the mug on the side table, she sat and tucked one foot under her.

Barkley plodded out of the bedroom and lay on the floor in front of the sofa.

"You miss Chloe, don't you, buddy?" Grace leaned over and scratched the Great Dane's head, and he licked her palm. "It's going to be okay. She'll be back soon, and you'll get all kinds of loving."

The dog yawned and laid his head down.

"Good boy. You get some rest while I work."

She clicked the icon to access the online database and typed in the password.

Please, Lord, let my hunch be wrong.

She clicked on the search box and typed Mountain Shadow. After the spinning circle stopped, she opened the medical history and read the toxicology report. All the drugs listed on the paper copy were listed in the electronic file, but someone had lowered the toxicity levels. A careless typo by the transcriptionist? She didn't think so.

Next, she opened the electronic copy of the necropsy report. Cause of death was listed as heart failure due to a ventricular septal defect. A hole in the heart. A defect the Thoroughbred would have been born with. Why would someone falsify the clinic's records? No, not why. Why was obvious. The stallion had died from an overdose of metabolism-enhancing drugs. Someone wanted to cover up the cause of death. The real question was who. The transcriptionist? One of the vet techs? James?

Barkley got up, went to the door, whimpered and then looked back at her.

"Do you need to go out, boy? Hmm?" Closing the laptop, Grace stood and stretched before crossing to the door. She patted Barkley's back and then reached for the handle. And paused, her hand on the knob. Evan had only allowed her to stay at the apartment if she agreed to remain inside with the doors locked at all times.

She looked out the window. The faintest hint of morning light had started to peek in the distance, but it would be another thirty minutes or longer before the sun rose.

The Great Dane whimpered and scratched at the door.

The clinic didn't open until seven, and the staff wouldn't arrive until a quarter till. Barkley could not wait hours to relieve himself. She sighed.

Though technically outside, the kennel was a fully enclosed, locked area accessed via a door from the main building. There was a small grassy area, so the Great Dane could do his business.

"Barkley, come." She snagged her cell phone off the coffee table and slipped it into her pocket.

Opening the door that led downstairs into the clinic, she allowed Barkley to take the lead, their steps guided only by the night-lights spaced randomly along the hallway. Her heart picked up tempo with every step she took, as if she were an intruder afraid of being caught. Pressing a hand against her chest, she puffed out a breath of air.

Grace wouldn't really be breaking her promise to Evan. She'd stay inside the doorway and wouldn't step outside. No one would see her.

"Okay, boy. Go." She opened the door and the Great Dane darted out into the kennel. Some of the boarded animals stirred and barked a greeting. Others lay undisturbed. Barkley went from cage to cage, sniffing the area.

"Hurry, boy. Do your business and let's get back upstairs."

Barkley ambled over to the grass then headed back in her direction, until something outside the fence caught his attention. He stood tall and regal, his ears straight up and his tail back, a low growl emanating from deep in his throat. The growl grew into a fierce bark, causing the hair on the nape of her neck to stand and goose bumps to pop up along her arms.

What had the animal seen? Did she dare go look? No, she'd watched enough horror movies to know that wouldn't end well. *Get back upstairs to safety and call the police.* That's what she would be yelling to the heroine on the television screen in this scenario.

She whistled softly. "Barkley, in."

The animal disregarded the command, his growling bark becoming more aggressive. She needed to get upstairs but didn't want to leave her sister's beloved pet behind.

Ignoring the internal voice silently screaming, *Don't do it*, she inched one foot in front of the other and took a few steps into the kennel, staying behind the cages.

Heavy footsteps crunched on the gravel outside the fence. Slipping her phone out of her pocket, she pressed speed dial, thankful Evan had programmed the important numbers into her phone before leaving last night.

"Come on, answer the phone." Grace bounced nervously from foot to foot as she counted the rings. *Two... three...*"Bark—"

"Blackberry Falls Police Department." An authoritative female voice sounded across the line.

"I'm at Porter Animal Clinic." Grace spoke barely above a whisper. "I need an officer. There's someone outside."

"Is this Dr. Porter?"

"Yes."

"Where are you in the building?"

"We're in the kennel."

"We? Who's with you?"

"My sister's dog."

"Find somewhere to hide and stay on the line. An officer is on the way."

The metal chain-link fence rattled. Was the person trying to climb into the kennel?

Grace's breath caught in her throat. She stumbled and clutched the bars of the cage closest to her. This drew Barkley's attention. He headed toward her and then stopped, turned and growled again.

Peering around the cage, she spotted a shadowy figure straddling the six-foot fence. He threw his leg over and dropped into the kennel.

"Barkley, come!" She turned and raced indoors.

For all his barking and growling, the Great Dane was as scared as Grace and stayed at her heels entering the building.

She slammed the door shut and locked it.

"The intruder's inside the fence!" She yelled into the phone. "Tell the officer to hurry."

The shadow man loomed on the other side of the frosted-glass door. The doorknob rattled. Barkley whimpered and headed for the apartment. Grace backed away, then turned and ran after Barkley.

"Dr. Porter. What's happening?"

The door busted open.

"He's inside." Her words came out in a husky whisper.

Her phone beeped and went silent. Dead battery. Grace slid the phone into her back pocket. And ran. Four more steps to the top of the stairs and her apartment.

He gained on her. Now, only a few steps below her.

Half turning, she grasped the rail, raised her leg and kicked as hard as she could. Her foot connected with his chest. The man stumbled and fell backward with a heavy thud.

He lay unmoving at the foot of the stairs, arms and legs spread-eagle, a ski mask hiding his identity. She itched to remove it to see his face, but she didn't dare get near him. What if he was only winded and not unconscious? As if to answer her unspoken question, the man groaned and started to push to his knees.

Grace turned and darted the rest of the way up the stairs. *Lord, please let help arrive in time.*

SIX

A ringing phone shattered the early morning quiet. Evan woke with a start and pushed himself up into a seated position. Snatching his cell off the nightstand, he checked the screen. Blackberry Falls PD.

He was on instant alert. "Bradshaw here."

"Chief. There was an intruder at Porter Animal Clinic." Reba Franklin, the night shift dispatcher, had his full attention.

"Is Grace okay?" Jumping out of bed, he put the phone on speaker, tossed it onto the bedside table and hurriedly pulled on a pair of jeans and a T-shirt.

"We think so, sir."

"What do you mean you think so?" Why was his dispatcher talking in circles? "Tell me what you know."

"Dr. Porter called the station approximately ten minutes ago. Someone was outside the kennel. They made entry. At that time, we lost communication with Dr. Porter."

Fear gripped him. Why had he left her there alone?

The dispatcher continued. "When Officer Wilkes arrived at the clinic, the side door was ajar. He entered the building. There were signs of a break-in and a struggle, but the intruder had fled the scene. Dr. Porter had barricaded herself in the apartment. She's shaken up and insists on giving her statement to you."

"Is Wilkes with her now?"

"Yes, sir."

"Tell him to stay with her. I'm on my way." Disconnecting, he tried Grace's cell, but the call went straight to voice mail. He shoved his feet into a pair of running shoes and bent to tie them. Then he grabbed his wallet and keys off the dresser before crossing to the nightstand and retrieving his service revolver from the locked box. Time to roll.

He walked into the hallway and froze. Camden. He'd call his mom from the car and let her know he needed to drop him off at her house.

Evan entered the small room decorated in a superhero theme. His path illuminated by a Spider-Man night-light, he stepped around the toy cars and plastic dinosaurs littering the floor.

Bending, he grabbed a pair of tennis shoes off the floor then scooped his still-sleeping, pajama-clad son up into his arms and headed for the garage.

"Where are we going?" Camden mumbled, his eyes still closed as Evan put him in the SUV.

"Grammy's house," Evan answered as he secured the seat belt across the booster seat.

His son's green eyes opened and peered at him accusingly. "You promised we'd go fishing today."

Evan groaned inwardly. He *had* promised, after missing the end of the school year picnic. Thankfully, school would be out for summer break soon, giving him one less thing to juggle.

"The day has just started." He ruffled Camden's hair, then climbed into the driver's seat and backed out of the garage. "First, you get to hang out with Grammy and

Poppy, have breakfast and watch cartoons. Then, when I get back, we'll go fishing."

You, me, Grace and Barkley. If she's okay. Please, let her be okay.

He desperately wanted to turn on the lights and sirens as he raced to her, but he didn't want to frighten Cam.

By the time they arrived at his parents' house, his son was wide-awake. His mother met them in the driveway, wearing her nightgown and housecoat. She opened the back door and unbuckled Camden, who, once free, raced into the house.

Libby Bradshaw poked her head through Evan's open window. "Don't worry about a thing, son. Cam's fine here as long as necessary. You take care of Grace and concentrate on finding the person trying to hurt her and her sister."

"Yes, ma'am." Having grown up in a military family, he always used "ma'am" and "sir" when talking to his parents. "And thanks, Mom."

She kissed his cheek and hurried indoors.

He may never have a wife and Camden may never have a mother in his life again, but they had his parents and Lisa's parents. Evan had spent too long feeling sorry for himself and focusing on past mistakes, maybe it was time he started counting his blessings instead of his failures.

Backing out of the drive, Evan flipped on the siren and sped toward Porter Animal Clinic and Grace.

He pulled into a parking spot beside the other patrol car and raced up the outside stairs that led to the apartment, ignoring the neighbors and community members gathering in clusters on porches and outside other businesses. It was natural for people to be curious and concerned when a police cruiser, or two, showed up outside

a residence or business, but Grace would hate all the attention.

Tom Wilkes, a twenty-four-year veteran of the force,
stood on the small deck outside the apartment. Evan
raised an eyebrow, and the older man shrugged. "She
wouldn't open the door. Insisted you were the only one
she'd talk to."

Evan clapped his officer on the shoulder and jerked
his head in the direction of the small crowd. "See if any
of the residents who live nearby saw or heard anything.
And while you're at it, try to persuade them to disperse."

"I'm on it." Wilkes ambled down the stairs and across
the street.

Knocking, he identified himself, saying, "It's Evan."

He held his breath and waited. Finally, the click of the
lock sounded, but the door remained closed. He puffed
out the breath, twisted the knob and stepped into the
apartment.

The tension he hadn't even known he'd been holding
since the phone call that woke him lifted from his shoulders at the sight of Grace. She was sitting on the same
green-plaid sofa they had sat on together the night before,
only now it blocked the door leading to the clinic. Barkley rested at her feet with his head in her lap, soaking
up the attention as she rubbed her hands over his head.

She glanced up, and her eyes shone when she saw him.
A wisp of blond hair fell in her face, which was makeup-
free, giving full exposure to the smattering of freckles
across her nose and cheeks. She looked both hopeful and
frightened at the same time, much like the twelve-year-
old girl she had been the first day he'd walked into sixth-
grade science class at Blackberry Falls Middle School.
She'd been happy that day to have the new kid assigned as
her partner because the experiment had made her queasy.

He remembered teasing her later that same day at lunch when she'd shared with him she wanted to be a veterinarian when she grew up. If only this incident could be laughed away as easily.

Evan crossed the small room and sat beside her. "Want to tell me what happened?"

"Barkley needed to go out. It was still two hours until any of the staff would arrive, and I couldn't make him wait." She focused on brushing her fingers through the animal's fur. "I know you told me to stay inside, but I thought the kennel would be safe."

Evan put two fingers under her chin and lifted her head until her eyes met his. He bent toward her, stopping himself mere inches from kissing her, his heartbeat echoing in his ears. Could she hear it? To cover his near faux pas, he pretended he was only close to emphasize his point. "I'm not mad at you. You didn't do anything wrong."

She nodded, but sadness emanated from her silver-blue eyes.

He sat back against the cushion. "Now, tell me everything."

Evan listened as she recounted the story, how the intruder jumped the six-foot chain-link fence and busted through the door. As she spoke, her voice trembled with fear, pulling him into the scene. He had no difficulty picturing her executing the roundhouse kick that had saved her life.

He smiled. "I guess those karate lessons finally paid off."

She looked at him blankly.

"Remember? In eighth grade, you went through a phase of wanting to be a PI and begged me to take karate with you. Six months later, you got bored and quit."

"I didn't even think of that. I just kicked and hoped I could get away."

He was thankful she had kept her wits about her and had done what was needed to escape harm.

"Did you get a good look at the guy? Could you identify him?"

A frown marred her face, and she shook her head. "He wore a mask."

"Don't tell me it had an animal face screen-printed on it."

"No. Not this time. This one was a solid dark color. I couldn't tell if it was black or navy."

He'd look at the clinic's security footage later, but for now, he wanted to give Grace time to process everything. He knew how her mind worked. If he left her alone, she'd sit there replaying everything over and over in her mind, getting angrier with herself for putting herself in the situation by leaving the apartment. However, if he encouraged her to talk about it, she'd process what had happened with a clear mind and let it go.

"What about height? Weight? Build? Anything at all."

"See, that's the thing bothering me the most. The guy seemed different this time. Maybe it's because I didn't get a clear view of him." She shooed Barkley away, and turned to face Evan, tucking one leg under her as she sat sideways on the sofa. "I'm not sure if it's because I froze during the attack on Chloe, watching everything play out in slow motion, and this time, I was running for my life. Whatever the reason, the guy seemed taller. Broader." She bit the corner of her lip, as if contemplating whether to continue.

"And?" he prompted.

"I didn't see his face, but he seemed more agile... younger."

Whatever he'd expected her to say, that wasn't it. Could this attack have been unrelated to the other two? Was it possibly a foiled burglary? Completely unrelated to the attack on Chloe?

His gut said no. That meant only one thing. More than one person wanted Grace dead.

"There's been no change. Your sister is stable, and we're keeping her comfortable." The nurse's words were disappointing, but Grace hadn't really expected Chloe's condition to improve overnight. Suppressing her frustration, she disconnected the call. Although she yearned to be in Denver with her sister, Grace knew Blackberry Falls was where she needed to be. For now.

Crossing to the small vanity table, Grace gathered her hair into a messy bun at the nape of her neck and secured it with an elastic hair tie. Then she finished her look with minimal makeup—tinted moisturizer, a light coat of brown mascara and a pale, natural lipstick. Touching her lips, her heart raced. She'd thought Evan was going to kiss her earlier. And if she were honest, she'd wanted him to.

With a sigh, she slipped her feet into comfortable sneakers and walked into the living room. Someone had moved the sofa back to its original spot, and Evan and an older officer were sitting at the small dining table in deep discussion.

She signaled for Barkley to follow her and headed to the door that led down into the clinic.

"Where are you going?" Evan's question halted her steps.

Grace turned to find him towering over her. Forcing a smile, she replied, "It's time to open the clinic."

"Oh, no, you don't." He took her arm and led her to a

corner of the small sitting area. "The clinic can remain closed for the day."

Twisting out of his grasp, she squared her shoulders and pulled herself to her full five-foot-nine height, ready for a fight. She would not disappoint her father, even if he wasn't around any longer to see it. "No, it can't. The clinic was closed yesterday with most of the appointments being rescheduled for today."

"I don't care. Your safety is of the utmost importance."

"I agree, and I'd very much like to stay alive. But these patients' lives are important, too."

"You can send the urgent cases to one of the three vet clinics in Lincoln Park, it's only a thirty-minute drive."

"Only one of the vet clinics in Lincoln Park is open on Saturdays, and they have their own patients to worry about."

"Too bad. You're not opening. I can't guarantee your safety if you do."

"Well, that is too bad, because I am opening the clinic today. If I were an MD, would you ask me to put my patients' lives in danger by postponing critical care?" He started to reply, but she rushed on before he could protest. "No, you wouldn't. Look, in addition to vaccines, there are two surgeries scheduled for today, an ACL repair on a nine-year-old greyhound and the removal of a mass on the liver of a twelve-year-old Burmese cat. These animals' lives are as important as mine. They're someone's family members. They're loved as much as any human, and I will not postpone their care."

Evan shoved a hand through his hair, frustration etched on his face. She hated to cause him to worry, but she'd taken an oath to provide the best care for any patient in her charge. And, whether she liked it or not, James's patients had become hers yesterday when he'd walked out of the clinic. Good thing she had already lined up several people, some newly graduated and some with experience, to interview as his replacement.

Actually, Grace planned to hire two veterinarians to replace James, not that he had done the work of two doctors, but the practice had been lacking. She'd hired someone to take up the slack after her father passed, but they'd only lasted three weeks before James had run them off, telling Grace and Chloe if they hired an extra veterinary assistant, he could handle the workload without another veterinarian.

If only she hadn't stayed away after her father's death… She might have been able to…to what? Stop James from being so controlling about the clinic? Save her sister's marriage?

"What time does the clinic close?"

"Um…what?" Lost in thought, Evan's words hadn't penetrated her consciousness.

"I asked what time the clinic closes."

"Oh. Ah, noon." Hope swelled inside her. "Then we're closed until eight o'clock Monday morning."

"Which gives you forty-eight hours to make other arrangements for the care of the animals of Blackberry Falls." He winked.

Unable to resist, she offered a saucy smile and replied, "Or it gives you forty-eight hours to find the person behind the attacks and put him in jail."

He sobered. "Believe me, that would be my preference. I'll do my best."

"Does this mean you won't fight me about working today?"

"It means I understand the importance of your work."

The older officer pushed away from the table and ambled over to them. "I can stick around and guard the doctor."

"Wilkes, you've just completed a night shift, you need to go home and get some rest."

"No, sir. I never go to sleep before one. Besides, Martha has gone to Albuquerque to visit our daughter and the grandkids, so I'll be going home to an empty house."

"Doesn't matter. I can't pay overtime. I'll pull a patrol officer to hang out here for the four hours needed."

"Well, sir, you do that, if you feel it's best." Wilkes turned to her and smiled. "Dr. Porter, since it's lonely at my house, would you mind if I come back here and spend a few hours hanging out with you and the animals after I've gone home and changed into civilian clothes?"

Evan watched the exchange, an amused expression on his face, and Grace knew he was awaiting her reply. Probably more than anyone, Evan knew she wasn't comfortable with people going out of their way doing things for her. How could she say no when he looked so proud that his officer had volunteered his free time?

She searched the older man's face. Something about the officer bothered her. She couldn't put her finger on it. Maybe it was the forced smile that didn't reach his eyes. She mentally shook herself.

What was wrong with her? Had she really started to suspect everyone? *Stop imagining things.* Evan trusted him. The man had worked the night shift. He's not being unfriendly, he's tired. Which might be a good thing. He could find a corner and sleep while she worked, and she could forget he was there. It wasn't like she needed a guard at the clinic anyway. The guy who was after her wouldn't make a move with her entire staff and clients present, would he?

SEVEN

Evan craned his neck for a better view of the exam room. The door was still closed. In the past hour, Grace had given vaccines to three dogs and one cat, and now she was stitching up a ferret brought in with a nasty-looking cut. The waiting area was empty for the moment but wasn't likely to stay that way for long.

Settling back into the vinyl chair, he glanced at the clock. It had been forty-five minutes since he'd sent Wilkes home to change out of his uniform and eat breakfast. The veteran officer should be back soon, then Evan could go to the station and follow up on leads.

In the meantime, he had gone over the security footage from the outside cameras, trying, to no avail, to identify the intruder. The man, or woman, had strategically avoided most of the cameras, and in the kennel where they couldn't be avoided, they had kept their back to them. Unfortunately, there were no cameras inside the clinic.

The bell over the door dinged, and Ben Hamilton came in with his Australian shepherd. He waved at the receptionist, Tina Layton, and headed into the waiting area. The animal tugged on his leash, trying to get to Evan for attention.

"No, Max. Stay," Hamilton commanded.

Evan laughed and stroked the dog between his ears as the older man stood looking on. "It's okay. He's just curious." The animal was a beauty, with one blue eye and one brown eye.

"Have you given any more thought to who may have driven that truck off your property the other night, Ben?" Evan asked casually once the man was settled in a chair.

"I've answered all of your officers' questions, chief. Multiple times. My answers haven't changed," the rancher replied without emotion.

Evan studied the man's weathered face. "I understand you've been trying to buy the Osborne farm."

"I tried to warn Chloe of the dangers of living on a farm alone. She should have listened to me."

"Did you have anything to do with the attack? Trying to scare her off?"

"The only thing I'm guilty of is offering advice to an old friend's daughter and trying to add to my acreage. And I will not sit here and be interrogated by you." The rancher pushed to his feet and walked over to the receptionist's desk, slamming his hand on the counter. "Cancel Max's appointment." Glaring at Evan, he added, "I'll take him to the vet in Cañon City for his shots."

Evan walked up to the counter. "Now, Ben, there's no need for that."

Ben harrumphed and led Max out the door, the Australian shepherd barking and straining at his leash when he spied a woman exiting her vehicle with a pet carrier.

Evan's cell phone rang, and he slipped it out of his pants' pocket. FBI Special Agent Randy Ingalls's number flashed on the screen.

Eight months ago, Agent Ingalls had approached Evan for his assistance. Working undercover, Ingalls had been trying to infiltrate an organization behind off-the-grid horse races in the county. Though the organizers always secured the appropriate permits for match races, Evan and Agent Ingalls both knew illegal activities such as substance abuse, including performance-enhancing drugs given to the animals, gambling, money laundering, and human trafficking were happening behind the scenes.

Evan had tried to reach the agent earlier. He crossed to the receptionist's desk, pointed to Chloe's office and mouthed, *I'll be in there.*

Tina smiled. "Go ahead, dear."

Evan settled into the desk chair, making sure he'd still have a good view of the exam room door, and answered his phone. "Ingalls, thanks for returning my call."

"No problem. I'd like to hear more about these attacks and why you think they're connected to the match races."

Evan quickly filled the agent in on the events of the past thirty-six hours.

A sick feeling settled in the pit of Evan's stomach. If the changes in the reports Grace found weren't a clerical error, someone connected to Porter Animal Clinic was involved in the illegal activities, too. Most likely providing the drugs being used on the horses. But was that person behind the attacks? Would someone who worked at the clinic be willing to kill the sisters to keep their involvement a secret? As a law-enforcement officer, he knew that answer was yes. Anyone who felt trapped was capable of murder.

"I'm trying to go undercover as security at the next race," Ingalls said. "Send me photos of the clinic's staff. If any of them show up at the race, maybe we can narrow down your suspects."

"I'll get them to you as soon as I get to the office." Evan picked up the files from earlier and flipped through them. "I'll also send you a copy of the toxicology report on the horse that died."

"What are you doing here, James?" Grace's harsh tone drew Evan's attention to the open exam room door. She was facing her brother-in-law, whose back blocked the door to Chloe's office, obscuring Evan's view.

Had James seen him looking over the files? Evan ended his call and slid the folders into a drawer. He pushed away from the desk and stood, quietly listening. Ready to intervene if needed.

"I came to do my job," James stated matter-of-factly.

"Walking out yesterday was your choice. What right do you have to be here now?" Grace peered over James's shoulder, meeting Evan's gaze.

Noticing the tired, almost defeated look in her eyes, Evan offered her an encouraging smile and a nod.

James spun around and glared. "I should have known your bodyguard would be here."

"I take my job seriously. Protecting the citizens of Blackberry Falls, even those who have been away for a while, is my job." Evan measured his words, speaking in a soft, even tone as he walked toward the pair. Stopping in front of James, he added, "I believe Grace asked you what you're doing here."

"Like I told her, I'm here to do my job." James's shoulders slumped, and he gave a half shrug before looking at Grace. "You may not like me, but these animals have been my patients for the past four years. Since we were closed yesterday, I rescheduled two surgeries for today. I figured you'd like help. I can do the surgeries while you see the other patients."

Was James being sincere or was he playing a game to keep a close eye on the investigation?

"I don't know…" Grace looked at Evan questioningly.

He shrugged, unable to give her guidance on this matter. Not that Evan would take any chances where Grace was concerned. She would not be left unprotected with James on the premises.

"If you want me to leave, I will," James said.

"No. It's okay. You're right. Having you complete a surgery would be helpful. The ACL repair will take the longest, so start with it. I'll take care of the scheduled vaccinations and the walk-ins. If I get finished before you, I'll do the other surgery."

James nodded assent, turned and walked toward the door marked Operating Room 1, stopping to say something to Valerie on his way. The vet tech laughed at whatever he'd said and glanced their way.

Grace turned back to Evan and whispered, "What do you make of James showing up today?"

He stepped back and motioned her into the office, closing the door after she'd entered. "I'm not sure. But I don't want you alone with him." He walked past her and crossed to the desk. "Officer Wilkes will need to be in close proximity of you at all times. Do you understand?"

"I'll make sure he has a seat with a clear view of the exam rooms."

Evan reached into the drawer and retrieved the folders. "I'm not sure if James saw me looking through these files or not, but I don't want to leave them where he might find them. Are you okay with me locking them in my car?"

"Normally, I wouldn't let medical records leave the clinic, but I don't see as we have any other choice at the moment." Grace hid a yawn behind her hand.

Up close, Evan could see the dark under-eye circles that she'd tried to conceal with makeup. He hated that she hadn't been able to sleep the night before. That made two nights with minimal sleep for her. If he accomplished nothing else today, he had to ensure she had a safe place to rest her head tonight.

When he'd called earlier to check on Chloe, he and Ryan had discussed the situation. The younger man had suggested Evan and Grace stay in the cabin overlooking the waterfall in the woods at the edge of his parents' property, the Flying V Ranch.

How would Grace take the suggestion? Like it or not, she wasn't staying at the clinic alone again. He'd also have to make arrangements for Camden to stay with his parents for the time being, but he wasn't worried about that. Cam would love getting to stay with Grammy and Poppy, fishing in the pond and eating Grammy's home cooking.

"Look, Grace, I think I have a safe place—"

"Dr. Porter?" Tina Layton poked her head around the door. "Your next patient is waiting in exam room three."

"I'll be right there." She turned back to him with an apologetic smile. "I've gotta go. Can we discuss this when you pick me up?"

"Sure. I'll be here by a quarter till." He followed her into the hall as he spoke. A dog barked in the waiting area, and Evan could see a golden Labrador retriever straining at his leash as Wilkes strolled down the hall toward them.

The officer nodded at Grace as she passed on her way to the exam room. Pride surged through Evan at the willingness of his men to donate their free time to protect the Porter sisters.

It was nice knowing he wasn't alone in the quest to keep Grace alive, but he struggled to squelch the uneasy feeling settling into the pit of his stomach at the thought of not being the one there protecting her.

* * *

Grace knelt and handed the fluffy, white rabbit to his owner, a young brown-haired girl with freckles scattered across her face. "Here you go, Daisy. Marshmallow is perfectly healthy, and he's ready to go home."

Grace glanced at her watch. Eleven twenty. Forty minutes until closing time, and she had seen the last scheduled patient.

"Is Dr. Osborne still in surgery?" she asked Tina, who was in the waiting area straightening the magazines.

"Yes. He finished the ACL repair on the greyhound." Tina moved to the collars and leashes display and continued with her organizing. "He's operating on the Burmese cat now."

Grace picked up a paper coffee cup someone had left sitting on the floor beside one of the brown vinyl chairs and disposed of it. "What time did he get started?"

"Around eleven."

"Did he say how long he thought it would take?" she asked as she reached to retrieve a chew toy that had fallen off the display on the counter.

"He expects to finish by noon." The older woman's smile reached all the way to her dark brown eyes, her brown hair styled in a short bob framed her face. "Go sit and rest a minute. I can finish straightening things. You've been on your feet all morning. I've left homemade blueberry muffins in the kitchenette, and there's a fresh pot of coffee."

The mention of food had Grace's stomach growling. She had forgotten to eat anything for breakfast. "Thank you, Tina. I'll be in Chloe's office if anyone needs me."

Officer Wilkes sat on a stool he'd placed at the end of the long reception desk. His vantage point gave him a clear view of the front door, the three exam rooms and the hall leading to the operating area.

"Come on," she said when she passed him. "Let's grab some coffee and muffins." Maybe nourishment would help erase the somber expression on the officer's face.

He followed her and soon they settled in chairs around the small table in the corner of her sister's office.

"Yum. That is probably the best blueberry muffin I've ever had," she said between bites.

"I could have told you that, ma'am. Ms. Tina always wins the blue ribbon at the fair for her baked goods."

Grace examined the man sitting across from her. Officer Wilkes had silver hair and blue eyes, his expression guarded. His wrinkled face was almost leathery, like a man who'd spent a lot of time outdoors. He seemed familiar, but she couldn't place him.

"Trying to figure out where you know me from?" he asked as if reading her mind.

"Actually, yes." No point trying to hide the fact that she couldn't remember all the people she'd known growing up, though most people would probably find it strange she didn't remember everyone since the population of the town was less than seven hundred.

"I guess you were about nine years old. You came with your daddy to make a house call at my place. I had a small farm—what people today would call a hobby farm—with a few goats, some chickens and some ducks. One of the goats had gotten his leg caught in some wire and needed stitches. I planned to load him up and bring him to the clinic, but when I called, Dr. Porter said it was closing time so he'd stop by on his way home." A smile lifted the corners of his mouth. "Your daddy always said it was less stressful for farm animals if he came to them, instead of them having to be brought to the clinic in trailers."

He met her eyes and the smile disappeared. "You were with your daddy that day. I think you had gone to the clinic after school. Anyway, you asked to see all the animals while he stitched up the goat."

"You gave me pellet food to feed the ducks," she interjected.

He nodded, a faraway expression on his weathered face. "I did."

A forgotten memory replayed in slow motion through her mind. "I tripped on a tree root and fell in the pond. You saved me."

"It was my fault for not watching you more closely."

The man's guilt at her carelessness saddened her. "You couldn't have known I'd fall in."

"I could have warned you and helped you avoid the accident." He placed his elbows on the table and leaned closer. "My advice for you, right now, to keep you from a disaster far worse than a dip in a pond, is to get in your vehicle and hightail it to Denver. And when your sister is released from the hospital, keep her there. Cut all ties with this town."

The hairs on her arms stood on end. Were his words a warning of concern or were they a threat?

Officer Wilkes smiled. "I'm sorry if that sounded mean, but I feel like I owe it to your daddy to step in and give fatherly advice since he's no longer around."

Before she could respond, Tina's voice sounded over Chloe's desk phone intercom. "Excuse me, Dr. Porter. Henry Green from Mountain View Ranch is on the line. His three-year-old Thoroughbred colt, Knight's Honor, is in distress."

She stood, dusted crumbs off her lap and crossed to the desk. "Thank you, I'll take the call in here."

"He's on line two."

Grace pushed a button, picked up the receiver and listened to Henry Green describe the horse's symptoms. Sweating profusely. Labored breathing. Listlessness. Mountain View Ranch? Henry and Olivia Green. They had been the owners listed on the necropsy report for Mountain Shadow.

"Mr. Green, are there any obvious signs of colic? Distended belly? Abdominal pain?"

"No. That was the first thing I checked."

Could Knight's Honor have been drugged, too? If so, the colt needed fluids to help flush the drugs out of his system.

She had to go with her gut. "Mr. Green, I'm on my way."

"Wouldn't you rather me bring him to you? That's how Dr. Osborne does things."

Grace bit back the retort that she wasn't Dr. Osborne. She was her father's daughter, and she'd treat the patients of Blackberry Falls the way he would have.

"No. I'll come to you." She met Officer Wilkes's gaze and smiled. "It'll be less stressful for Knight's Honor. In the meantime, see if you can get him to drink water. Don't give him anything else, just water. Got it?"

The gasp on the other end of the line had her questioning her decision. "If it's colic, water could rupture his stomach."

"And if my instincts are right, we're racing against time, and it could be the only thing that saves him." She hung up before he could respond and turned to the man standing at her elbow. "Officer Wilkes, I've got to make a house call."

"I don't think the chief would approve."

"That can't be helped. This is an emergency. If you

want to come, that's fine, but I understand if you need to get home."

"No, ma'am. I'm not letting you out of my sight."

"You can call Evan while I gather what I need. Let's go." After informing Tina where she was going, she retrieved the keys to the clinic's rigged-out truck, equipped to handle most emergencies. Then she gathered a variety of IV bags and headed out the side door.

While Officer Wilkes tried to reach Evan, Grace stowed the supplies in one of the metal storage boxes along the side panel of the truck bed.

"The desk officer said the chief was on the phone and had left orders to not be disturbed unless it was an emergency. Since it's not, I asked the officer to give him a message telling him where we're headed."

She pulled out onto the highway and headed north. "Sounds like you did all you could do. I don't think he'll be too mad, though. It's not like I'm going off somewhere unprotected, you're with me."

The older gentleman frowned, as if he wasn't convinced Evan would be okay with the situation.

"Well, I trust you to take care of me. After all, you saved my life when I was nine."

Henry Green had truly sounded upset. She would not leave an animal to die because of her own fears.

Please, Lord, I pray I'm not driving into a trap.

"Take the next left. In about a mile, the entrance to Mountain View Ranch will be on the right. You'll see two large stone columns and a double wrought iron gate with horse silhouette cutouts."

Grace followed the instructions as Officer Wilkes directed, thankful for his guidance. The landscape had changed more than she had expected in the fifteen years since she'd left the area.

"This is it." Wilkes pointed to the gates that stood wide-open, awaiting their arrival.

Turning onto the asphalt drive lined with fenced pastures, she followed the road for a half mile, passing a two-story, lodge-style log home before ending at a massive post-and-beam barn.

Grace parked the truck next to the tall, open double doors. Other than the new entrance at the road, nothing about Mountain View Ranch had changed. With rolling hills and green pastures that looked like a postcard come to life, it was still one of the most beautiful places in Blackberry Falls.

A man in his early seventies strode out of the barn to meet them, a serious expression on his face. His hair had turned almost solid white and his face had a few more wrinkles than she remembered, but Grace would have recognized Henry Green anywhere.

His ranch had been one of the places she'd most loved going with her dad. As a child visiting the ranch, the Greens had allowed her to feed apples to the horses, skip rocks in the pond behind the main house, and climb the big oak tree that stood on the hill behind the horse barn. Nothing she'd ever done had upset Henry Green. Having married late in life, he and his wife, Olivia, had never had children. One might have expected he would have been like some of her father's other clients who didn't have patience for a curious child, but Henry had always been a laid-back person who didn't get riled easily.

The elderly man pulled her into a quick hug the moment she stepped out of her vehicle. "Grace Porter, it's good to have you home. Your daddy would be so proud that you're working at his clinic."

Her heart constricted at his words, and her throat tightened as tears stung her eyes. Her number one goal growing up had been to make her daddy proud, that was the main reason she'd followed him around begging to go on house calls the summer between third and fourth grade. The other reason had been her two-year-old sister at home, constantly following her around and getting into her things.

Henry moved back and commanded, "Now, grab your supplies and let's save my colt."

Grace quickly collected the items she'd brought with her as Officer Wilkes stood to the side talking to Henry. If the ranch owner wondered why she had an off-duty officer with her, he never let on. But why would he wonder when the gossip mill of Blackberry Falls had no doubt filled in every community member on the plight of the Porter sisters.

Her arms full, she nodded at the barn entrance. "Lead the way."

The interior aisle of the barn was more than a hundred feet long and lined with stalls on both sides. The lower half of each stall had been constructed of tiger wood, a strong hardwood that would be difficult for a spirited horse to kick and splinter. The upper half was constructed of a matte-black, powder-coated steel railing.

"It's awfully quiet around here," Wilkes commented.

"That's because we only use this barn for injured animals and foals. Got a bigger barn a little ways past this one. The ranch hands are out there now setting up a race between a couple of colts and a filly. You'll probably hear them in a bit, when they get started."

Henry paused outside a stall a third of the way down the aisle. Grace looked over the top railing and saw a magnificent chestnut colt with a white blaze lying listlessly in the corner, his labored breathing echoing in the small space.

"Did you give him water?" she asked as she followed the rancher into the stall. Officer Wilkes closed the door behind them and waited on the other side.

Henry nodded solemnly and patted the horse's shoulder. "He drank about half a gallon then collapsed here and hasn't moved again."

Grace examined the animal. No signs of trauma and no obvious signs of colic. His heart beat fast and erratically. She pulled a needle, a stabilizer and two Vacutainer blood collection vials from the equine medical bag she'd brought with her.

"Can you get on the other side and help hold him?" She waited for Henry to comply. Even though the horse was lethargic, she didn't want to risk his jerking upward and injuring himself or her.

Once the animal was secure, she pressed her thumb against the base of his long neck so the jugular vein would bulge. It took longer than it should have for the vein to fill with blood, an indication the Thoroughbred may be dehydrated. Inserting the needle, Grace drew two tubes of blood. After she'd completed that task, she started a one-liter bag of IV fluid. Slipping an S-hook through the small hole in the top of the bag, she handed it to the rancher to hook onto the hay feeder.

"Are you still ruling out colic?" Concern laced his voice.

She nodded and continued administering care to the distressed animal.

"What do you think it is?"

"I think he's had an overdose," she replied softly. "But we won't know if it's from the same drugs that killed Mountain Shadow until we get the labs back."

Grace met the ranch owner's gaze, anger burned in his hazel eyes. He didn't look like a man who had drugged his own horse.

"I was told Mountain Shadow died of a heart defect. Why that sorry, no-good, lying swindler!" Henry exploded.

"Who?"

"Never you mind. You concentrate on saving my horse." Pushing past Officer Wilkes, Henry exited the stall and headed down the aisle of the barn, his footsteps fading after he entered the office next to the tack room and slammed the door shut.

It was obvious Henry Green wasn't behind the drugging, but he knew who was. Grace looked at Wilkes and nodded toward the back of the barn. "Follow him and see if you can find out who he thinks did this."

"No way. The chief will have my hide if I let you out of my sight. I'll question Green when he gets back." The officer leaned against the stall door and crossed his booted feet at the ankles in a stubborn stance.

"You know, Wilkes, whoever drugged this horse is most likely the same person who attacked me. Finding out their name *is* the best way to protect me." She pushed to her feet and peered around him to look down the hall at the closed office door. "Go. Talk to him." When he raised an eyebrow and didn't budge, she added, "What could happen? You'll be less than fifty feet away."

EIGHT

Evan tapped a few keys on his laptop and hit Send.

"Okay, I emailed you the photos and bios of the employees of Porter Animal Clinic," he said into the phone.

"Great. I'll study them tonight, while I'm waiting for the phone call from the temp agency," Randy Ingalls replied.

Evan prayed the agent's plan to be hired as a security guard for the match race became a reality. "Do you know which ranches are taking part in the race tomorrow?"

"According to my source, there are a total of six. Two from Colorado Springs, one from Beulah Valley, one from Westcliffe, and two from Blackberry Falls…let me see." Evan heard papers rustle on the other end of the line. "Hamilton Thoroughbred Ranch and Mountain View Ranch."

"Hamilton Ranch was where Chloe Porter's attacker jumped in a truck and lost Lieutenant Johnson. My men have been out there twice since the attack. The Hamiltons claim not to have seen anything, and neither they nor their hired hands could—or would—identify the truck or who it belonged to."

"Could you send someone in to work undercover?"

"Not likely. The downfall of running a police station

in a small community is that everyone knows all the officers." Evan propped his elbows on the desk. "Of course, everyone knowing our officers can be an advantage, too, as it can lead some people to open up and tell us things. We'll continue to work on that. Let us know if you need our help with anything on your end."

"Sounds good. In the meantime, keep a close eye on Dr. Porter. If you're right and the evidence she found ties back to the group running the match races, the target on her back will only get bigger by the minute. These people don't play around, and they won't take a chance on losing what they've built here."

"Yeah, I know." Evan puffed out a breath and reached to shut down his computer.

He ended the conversation, asking the agent to keep him in the loop. It was noon, and he had promised Grace he'd be back at the clinic fifteen minutes ago. Pushing away from his desk, he headed out his office door.

"Chief!" Officer Lane Newman called out when Evan walked past the dispatch room. "I have a message for you from Wilkes."

Evan's steps faltered, and he did an about-face, striding over to the desk and accepting the piece of yellow memo paper the rookie held in the air.

For: Chief Bradshaw
From: Officer Tom Wilkes
Time: 11:32
Message: Headed to Mountain View Ranch with Dr. Porter for a house call.

Mountain View Ranch. Agent Ingalls's voice echoed in Evan's mind.

The message had been left thirty minutes earlier.

"Why am I just now getting this? You should have notified me when the call came in."

The rookie shrugged. "You left orders not to be disturbed. I asked if it was an emergency. Officer Wilkes said it wasn't and to give you the message before you headed to the clinic."

"Get Wilkes—" He swallowed the rest of his command. Wilkes was off duty. He wouldn't have his radio. Evan's determination to keep his department from going over budget had put Grace in danger.

He pulled his cell phone out of his back pocket and hit a speed dial number. The call went straight to voice mail. "Wilkes, call in ASAP."

He disconnected and tried Grace's number. Voice mail.

Wadding up the yellow paper and tossing it on the desk, he turned and raced outside to his vehicle. What if his officer and Grace had been ambushed?

Grace pulled the earpieces from her ears, draped the stethoscope around her neck and ran her hand along the Thoroughbred's flank. His pulse had become less erratic and his breathing less labored. The fluids seemed to be working, and the toxins were being flushed out of his body. Still, she needed to contact Dr. Underwood at the Anderson Vaughn Equine Hospital in Pueblo West to let him know the animal would be transported to his hospital for further observation.

Grace slipped her cell out of her pocket. Ugh. No service. Another downside of small-town living. She'd have to find a spot with a stronger signal. Sliding her hand along the blaze that ran from Knight's Honor's forehead to his muzzle, she leaned in and whispered, "We're going to make you all better."

The colt neighed softly, and she kissed him, his hair tickling her nose. "I'll be right back, boy."

Slipping out of the stall, Grace headed for the main entrance. Her sneaker-clad feet barely made a sound on the concrete floor. The barn was eerily quiet except for the murmur of conversation coming from the office. She prayed Henry Green was opening up to Wilkes about who he suspected of drugging the horses and why.

Once outside, she checked her phone again. A weak signal but not nearly strong enough. She needed to hear Dr. Underwood, and he needed to hear her. Rounding the corner of the barn, she saw the oak tree still standing proud and tall on its hill overlooking the barn. Hmm. It couldn't hurt to see if a slightly higher elevation would improve cell reception.

"How's Knight's Honor?"

Grace jumped at the sound of a woman's voice behind her.

Turning, she saw Olivia Green headed in her direction, a wicker basket clutched in her perfectly manicured hand. In her mid- to late-sixties, wearing a royal blue pantsuit with her platinum blond hair perfectly coiffured, Olivia looked like she'd walked off a fashion runway. A socialite from New York who'd given up high society for small-town life when she married, Olivia Green had always been the most elegant woman in Blackberry Falls.

"He's stabilized." Grace lifted her phone. "I'm trying to call the equine hospital to let them know to expect him."

"Cell reception is horrible in this area. I've been after Henry for years to get some kind of booster antenna or something to help. But he said there's no point since we still have landlines." The older woman reached Grace's side and leaned in to kiss the air near her cheek. "Grace, it's so good to have you home."

"Thank you, Mrs. Green. It's nice to see you."

"Why don't you go back in and use the phone in Henry's office?"

Grace shrugged. "He and Officer Wilkes are in there talking. I didn't want to disturb them."

"Okay, dear. I understand." Olivia raised the basket she carried. "It's well past lunchtime, and I know Henry hasn't eaten a thing, so I brought you all some sandwiches and fruit."

"That was sweet of you."

"It was nothing. A woman likes to feel like she's contributing when there's a crisis, and I like to feed people." The woman waved her hand dismissively. "Now, go make your call. I'll peek in on Knight's Honor before going back to the house. And I'll leave this basket on the bench outside his stall."

Grace hiked up the hill, taking in the view of the farm around her. She noticed the newer, larger barn farther back on the property. There was a large training area adjacent to it. Several onlookers watched as three horses with riders prepared to race inside the arena. It looked like the Greens had built a successful horse breeding and training business since she'd left Blackberry Falls.

A smile tugged at her lips. From the outside, Henry and Olivia Green seemed like an odd couple. He was a no-nonsense, down-to-earth man, most comfortable in blue jeans and boots. The total opposite of his wife. But they doted on each other and had always seemed to have a strong marriage.

A moment of sadness washed over her. Would she and Evan have had a marriage like the Greens' if she had stayed in Blackberry Falls instead of running like the scared woman-child she'd been? No sense fretting over it, since she'd never know.

Raising her phone, she checked the screen. Good, she had service. Clicking through her contacts, she moved closer to the tree to lean against the trunk. When she did so, she connected with something solid, but not hard like a tree. Startled, she whirled around and came face-to-face with the man who had attacked Chloe and wanted Grace dead.

A lost memory from long ago flashed in her mind's eye. She recognized him, but his name escaped her.

Grace stepped backward, stumbling on a root. She wobbled but somehow managed to maintain her footing while never breaking eye contact. A scream burned in her throat, begging for release, but when she opened her mouth, no sound came out. This couldn't be happening. It was broad daylight. There were people around. Someone had to see them on the hillside.

"Why are you so shocked to see me, Amazing Grace?" The man sneered. "I told you, you're next."

Like a starting pistol signaling the beginning of a race, his words spurred her into action. She turned and charged back down the hill, her screams drowned out by the crowd cheering the horses in the arena.

Evan activated the blinker and turned onto the private drive that wound through the Mountain View Ranch property. He had finally spoken with Officer Wilkes a few minutes ago. They were both in the barn. Grace was providing medical care for a horse that had possibly been drugged, and Wilkes was getting a list of suspects from Henry Green.

Grace was safe.

Still, the knot in Evan's stomach wouldn't loosen until he laid eyes on her.

Following the drive, he pulled around the main house to the original barn and slammed on his brakes. Grace was running down the hillside beyond the barn, a man pursuing her. The assailant grabbed her ponytail and dragged her back toward the trees.

Evan turned on the siren. Grace's captor spared him a quick glance and then tugged harder. Grace clawed at her attacker's hands. *Keep fighting, Gracie. Keep fighting.*

Evan pressed the accelerator, the SUV bouncing over the uneven terrain as he drove toward the pair. In the rearview mirror, he caught a glimpse of Wilkes running out of the barn. The Greens were close behind.

Shoving the gearshift into Park, Evan vaulted from the vehicle. The assailant slipped an arm around Grace's neck and held her like a shield.

Evan's hand hovered over his service revolver. The thought of using his weapon and possibly hitting Grace with a stray bullet made him hesitate. "Let her go!"

"Yeah, right." The man tightened his grip. Grace gasped for air, her face reddening.

Evan unsnapped his holster and stepped forward. "I said. Let. Her. Go."

Grace's attacker laughed and shoved her. She barreled into Evan. His arms instinctively went around her, but the power of the impact sent them both hurtling backward, tumbling down the incline. When they stopped, midway down the hill, he glanced back to the top. The man had vanished.

Officer Wilkes reached them. "Are you okay?"

"Yes. Go! Get him!" Evan commanded, his arm tightening around Grace, not wanting to let her go. Her face was buried in his chest.

"I'm sorry. I needed to call the animal hospital… Knight's Honor." She sobbed. "I thought I would be safe."

"Shh," he murmured. "It's okay. You're safe."

She pulled out of his arms, leaving him feeling suddenly empty.

"Because of you," she said. "You saved my life."

This time. But could he keep her alive?

Evan pushed to his feet, aware of the crowd gathered at the base of the hill. "Are you okay? Can you walk?"

She nodded. "I think so."

Taking her hand in his, he helped Grace to her feet and led her up the incline to his patrol vehicle, its engine still running. He settled her in the passenger seat. Closing the door, he leaned against the side of the SUV and radioed Dispatch for backup. When he finished, he contacted the county sheriff's office to request the K-9 unit be sent to help with the search.

Wilkes jogged up to the vehicle. "Sorry, Chief. He was gone before I entered the woods. I looked around but couldn't find his trail."

"How is that possible?" Evan demanded. "He couldn't have had more than a fifteen-second head start."

He studied his officer. Had the attacker really disappeared that quickly? Why had Wilkes left Grace alone? Was he working with the attacker? No. Evan squashed those thoughts. He trusted his officer with his life. He couldn't believe he'd be involved in anything that would harm Grace or Chloe.

Grace rolled down the window to listen to their conversation. Evan took in her pale complexion and the concern in her eyes. He hated to let her out of his sight, but he needed to work quickly to find her assailant before he came after her again. Attacking in broad daylight with other people around was a sign of desperation.

"I'm sorry, Grace. I never should have left your side," Wilkes apologized.

"You're right, you shouldn't have." Evan turned on his officer. "If you ever put her in danger again, it will be your last day on the force. Do you understand?"

"Yes, sir," Wilkes replied, not breaking eye contact.

"It's not his fault. I'm the one who convinced him it was okay."

Evan took a deep breath. It did matter. His officer had been careless. He had to catch the guy. Puffing out the breath, he said, "Take Grace someplace safe. I don't care if it's the barn or the main house, as long as you guard her and keep the crowd away from her."

"What about you?" Grace asked, fear audible in her voice.

He turned to her. "I'll be there after I get the K-9 unit in the woods. We've got to find the man's trail."

"I know him!" Grace gasped and her eyes widened. "When I saw him, this time, I thought he looked familiar. His name is Avery Hebert."

"Are you sure?" Wilkes asked.

She nodded. "Yes. It's been over twenty years since I last saw him. That's why I didn't recognize him at first."

"Hebert?" Evan questioned. "Is he related to Ralph and Lydia Hebert?"

Evan knew the Heberts. Ralph had had to quit his job in construction after being diagnosed with Parkinson's a few months ago, leaving Lydia to support the family on her salary as a school lunchroom worker.

"Avery is their oldest son," Wilkes answered. "He was irresponsible when he was younger, in and out of trouble with the law on a regular basis." The officer scrunched his brow. "As I recall, after he graduated high school, he got a job at a farm in Rockvale, and he seemed to have straightened out his life. Then a couple of years later, he got arrested for a DUI while transporting a horse to auction. He lost his job, and then he took off. I heard he went to Wyoming."

"Well, he's back now," Grace said in a matter-of-fact tone.

"So you say," said Wilkes. "We haven't officially ID'd him."

"But I know it was him."

Evan squeezed her hand. "It's okay. We'll catch him." Turning back to Wilkes, he added, "Now, get her someplace safe."

"I really need to go to the barn to make sure Knight's Honor is ready to be transported to the hospital," Grace insisted.

"Fine. As long as you're not planning to be the one transporting him."

"Oh, no. Henry will transport. I just need to check the Thoroughbred once more to make sure he's stabilized."

"Okay. Wilkes, drive Grace to the barn in my vehicle and don't leave her side."

"Are you sure you wouldn't rather me stay and search and have someone else guard Dr. Porter?"

To be honest, after what happened, Evan would have preferred to have another officer guard Grace, but he didn't have a lot of options at the moment. Besides, he needed to be able to trust his officer. He opened his mouth to reply, but Grace beat him to it.

"What happened to me wasn't your fault. You told me not to leave the area." She frowned. "I was careless. I'm sorry."

Evan clapped Wilkes on the shoulder. "I trust you. But don't let her slip away from you again."

"No worries there," Grace assured him. "I'm not about

to get out of his sight. I don't want another run-in with Avery."

Two Blackberry Falls police cruisers came up the drive with the county K-9 unit close behind, lights flashing.

Time to locate Grace's assailant. Assuming he was still on the ranch. If they couldn't find him, it would be time to hide Grace in a safe place. Evan hoped she wouldn't put up a fuss.

"I don't need to be driven back to the barn. It's a two-minute walk," Grace protested.

"My patrol car is right here. There's no need in you walking through the crowd to get back to the barn." Evan's tone was firm, indicating he wouldn't listen to any arguments.

He was right. The crowd watching the race had gathered when the commotion started.

Officer Wilkes drove her back to the barn, and Henry Green directed them to park inside, two employees closing the massive doors to stop prying eyes. Then, the rancher placed several of his men, armed with shotguns, at the various entrances to the barn.

If the armed guards on the outside weren't enough, Officer Wilkes stood less than ten feet from Grace, like a sentry guarding a fort, at full attention, observing the surroundings, his back to the stall.

Grace's hands shook as she worked, adrenaline still coursing through her veins from the recent attack. Taking a few steadying breaths, she worked to complete the task of unhooking the IV and prepping Knight's Honor for transfer. Once finished, she ran her hand the length of the colt's neck, leaned in and placed her cheek against his. "You will feel all better soon."

Stepping back, she called out, "Okay, Mr. Green.

Knight's Honor is ready to go." She exited the stall as one of the ranch hands entered.

Grace handed the small zippered bag to Henry. "These are the blood samples I drew when I first arrived. Dr. Underwood is expecting them. He said he'd have the results for us by Monday."

He accepted the bag, a look of concern on his face.

"Don't worry. Your colt's going to be okay. You did everything right, calling me as quickly as you did. And Dr. Underwood is one of the best."

"Thank you. For everything." The rancher looked down, unable to meet her eyes. "I'm sorry about Avery."

She sucked in a breath. "You knew he was the one who attacked Chloe? Is he the person you went to call?"

"I did try to call Avery, but I didn't know he attacked Chloe or was after you." Henry shook his head, and Officer Wilkes stepped closer, listening in. "One of my ranch hands saw you struggling on the hill with Avery and was headed to help you when Chief Bradshaw showed up. When you told me Mountain Shadow had been drugged and you thought Knight's Honor had been, too, I suspected Avery was the one who was responsible."

"Why would Avery Hebert drug your horses?" Evan asked, walking into the barn.

Henry moved the basket of uneaten food and sat on the bench outside Knight's Honor's stall, his shoulders slumped. "Because I'm a sucker for a sob story, and I thought maybe he'd grown up and changed his ways."

"That tells me why you hired him, not why he'd give drugs to your horses. Was he planning to run this horse in the match race tomorrow?"

"Yes. At first, I was against it since Mountain Shadow died following the last race. But the necropsy report said he died of a heart defect. So, I let Avery talk me into allowing Knight's Honor to run tomorrow."

"So what exactly goes on at these races?"

Henry looked Evan in the eyes. "I don't know. I haven't attended one. When Mountain Shadow ran, I was in the hospital recovering from knee replacement surgery."

Grace had heard about the unsanctioned horse races taking place across the state. There had been many news reports about the horses being given performance-enhancing drugs, as well as the illegal gambling and human trafficking that went along with these races. She'd had no idea off-the-grid match races had invaded Freemont County.

"Why would you want a horse to run in an unsanctioned race?" she asked before she could stop herself, not meaning to take over Evan's questioning.

"That was my next question." Evan leaned against a post.

"I knew better. I read the news reports about the illegal activities surrounding them, though the races themselves aren't illegal. Avery convinced me it would be an opportunity to see how our colts competed against horses they hadn't trained with. I figured there was no harm. I knew I wouldn't let anyone drug my horses." Sadness seeped into the rancher's voice. "I can't believe I allowed it to happen twice. I knew in my gut Mountain Shadow had been drugged, but the necropsy report said otherwise."

"Someone falsified it." Grace hated to admit the second part of that truth, but she knew she had to be honest. "Someone at the clinic."

Henry jerked his head upward. "Who?"

"I don't know." Anger rose like bile burning inside her. If news spread about the falsified records, it could destroy the business her father had built. Grace could not let that happen. "But you have my word, I won't stop until I find out the truth."

NINE

After leaving Mountain View Ranch, Evan had followed Grace back to the clinic so she could return the truck and pack a few necessities for herself and Barkley. He'd tried to convince her to let someone else take care of the Great Dane for a few days, but she'd insisted that the animal had to stay with her. Evan had caved to her wishes because he understood her desire to do anything she could to feel like she was helping Chloe.

Now, hours later, Evan sat on a blanket beside the pond on his parents' property packing the remnants of the picnic his mom had provided for their dinner. Once finished, he placed everything in the cargo space of his SUV. He was forever thankful to live close to his family and to always have their support. When he'd called earlier to ask his parents if they could watch Camden, they hadn't questioned him or thought twice about disrupting their normal day-to-day lives to care for their six-year-old grandson for an indefinite period.

Evan prayed it wouldn't be more than a day or two, but until they captured Avery Hebert and the threat against Grace was over, he would devote his time to keeping her safe. And he couldn't have Camden in harm's way.

"That's it… Keep reeling… You've got it," Grace

cheered for Camden as he worked to land the fish on his line. Barkley ran into the pond, barking at the fish splashing in the water.

Evan rushed to his son's side, and Grace got Barkley back onto the bank. Camden's little hand gripped the handle tightly as he spun it round and round. "Not so fast…that's it. You're doing great, son."

Finally, the fish was in the air. "Look at him, Dad! Isn't he a big one?"

"He sure is." Evan reached for the end of the line and pulled the largemouth bass in close, intent on setting him free.

"Hang on. Let me get a picture." Grace pulled her phone from her pocket.

Evan knelt beside Camden, and they both held the fishing line, the bass dangling between them, while Grace snapped a few pictures. He and Camden had been fishing together many times, but he'd never thought to take pictures. Evan was glad Grace had suggested it. He needed to do a better job of preserving memories with his son.

"How much do you think he weighs, Dad?"

"Hmm." Evan made a show of gauging its weight. "I'd say at least six pounds, seven ounces."

"You're silly, Dad." Camden giggled as Evan pretended to have difficulty lifting the fish.

"Time to set this little guy free." Evan gently removed the wiggling bass from the hook and lowered him back into the pond. He ruffled Camden's hair. "Okay, kiddo, I think it's time to load up and get you back to Grammy and Poppy's house."

"Can't we stay thirty more minutes?" Camden pleaded.

"Not today, son. It's already getting late. By the time I get you back to Grammy's and you get a bath, it'll be your bedtime."

"But, Dad, I want to spend more time with Barkley and Grace."

Evan lifted an eyebrow at his son's use of an adult's first name. He'd raised him to show respect to his elders.

She leaned in and whispered, "I told him he could call me Grace. I hope that's okay."

Evan hoped so, too. But he feared his son getting attached to her. When this was all over and she walked out of their lives, he didn't want a brokenhearted child.

The sun setting on the horizon cast orange and purple streaks in the sky, illuminating the small log cabin overlooking a waterfall on the edge of the Flying V Ranch. Set back off the road, the original Vincent family homestead was the perfect place to hide from prying eyes, though Grace wasn't sure why Ryan and Bridget's parents were willing to let her stay on their property.

She doubted anyone could find her there, but she couldn't be sure her presence wouldn't bring harm to the Vincents or their property. "Are you sure this is a good idea?"

"Yes," Evan answered. "It's a secluded spot few people know about, which is hard to find in our little town."

"You're right." She lifted her suitcase out of the back of his Jeep Wrangler—secretly thankful he'd decided to switch from his police vehicle after dropping Camden off—and followed Evan into the cabin. He placed the large bag of dog food he'd carried in onto a kitchen chair before heading back outside.

Barkley sniffed his new surroundings then plopped down on the rug in front of the rock fireplace. The main room of the cabin had an open-concept kitchen and living room. Leading off the living room, there was a short hallway with two doors. One was a small bedroom with a white, full-size, antique iron bed, an oak dresser and a matching side table with a lamp. The other door led to an updated bathroom with a claw-foot tub, a gray mosaic tile floor and a pedestal sink.

"What do you think?" Evan called from the main living area.

"I think it's very nice of Ryan's parents to allow us to use their cabin," Grace answered, retracing her steps down the hall. She looked at the duffel bag in his hand. "Do you really think it's necessary for you to stay here with me?"

Grace wasn't used to sharing living quarters with anyone. She'd lived alone since her junior year of college.

"I do." He tossed the duffel on the floor next to the sofa. "I'll sleep here, and you can have the bedroom."

The set of his jaw told her there would be no persuading him to change his mind. Wandering into the kitchen, Grace idly opened cabinet doors. The small pantry seemed well stocked, cans of homemade soups, vegetables and preserves lining the shelves. Opening the refrigerator, she noticed someone had stocked it with milk, eggs, fruit, cheese and a variety of lunch meat.

"Here's a note." Evan pulled a piece of paper from the thumbtack holding it in place on the corkboard attached to the side of the fridge. "'I tried to stock up on the necessities. If you can think of something I've left off the list or need anything at all, let me know, and I'll get it for you. We're praying for your safety and Chloe's healing. Mrs. V.'"

"That was thoughtful of her." Grace wasn't used to others doing so much for her. Back in Denver, she only knew the name of one of her neighbors.

"Yes, it was," Evan agreed, placing the note on the old butcher-block countertop. "It's getting late. Maybe you should go to bed. You've had a long day that started way too early."

"Actually, if you don't mind, I'd rather talk about Avery for a few minutes. I can't believe I've known who Chloe's attacker was this entire time."

"Technically, you didn't know this entire time. It took a specific event to jar your memory." He crossed the room and knelt in front of the fireplace. "Could you tell me what was different about today's attack that helped you remember?" he asked as he pulled kindling out of the metal bucket on the hearth and arranged it under the logs so he could start a fire.

Grace sat on the sofa and tucked her feet under her. "I think it was the way he looked at me. When I was younger, he'd call me 'princess,' but he'd have such a look of disgust on his face I always knew he meant it as an insult. He had that same look today."

She shivered, whether from the topic they were discussing or the cool night air, she wasn't sure, but she would be glad once Evan had a roaring fire warming the place. Pulling a soft, blue throw off the back of the sofa, she tucked it around herself.

"Why do you think he would do that?" Evan asked.

"I always thought it was because his family was poor and he thought I was a spoiled kid. We weren't rich by any means, but we had nice things. The first time it happened, I was in the clinic parking lot, riding the new, lime-green, ten-speed bicycle I had gotten the day before for my birthday."

"What was he doing at the clinic?"

"Dad had given him a part-time job. I believe it was his senior year of high school. One night, I overheard Dad telling Mom that Avery was great with the animals, and if he'd let go of some of his anger at the world, he'd have a bright future."

"Wilkes mentioned Avery had a troubled childhood. Do you know what he meant?"

"Avery had several run-ins with the law. He liked to party, and that included abusing drugs and alcohol. After he went to work for Dad, he seemed to sober up. Then when he graduated high school, Dad helped him find a full-time job at a ranch working with horses. But like Wilkes said earlier, that didn't last.

"When Avery got out of jail, he came by the clinic. I was in the kennel playing with the puppies, and I heard him talking to Dad. He wanted his old job back, but Dad told him he wouldn't hire him unless he agreed to go to an AA meeting. Avery said he didn't need AA. Dad told him he couldn't have an alcoholic around his daughters."

"And you never saw him again?"

"Not until the night he pushed Chloe over the balcony and threatened me."

"Then seems to me, I need to do some digging to figure out what led him to that place at that moment in time."

"You mean besides wanting to murder my sister and me?"

The morning sun illuminated the kitchen enough for Evan to search for coffee and filters.

He opened a drawer beside the sink, but it held dishcloths and dish towels. When he opened the next drawer, a high-pitched squeak echoed in the quiet house. He carefully closed the drawer, praying the noise hadn't awakened Grace. It had been nearing midnight before she'd finally gone to bed, and he had no way of knowing if she'd drifted off to sleep as easily as he had, complete exhaustion claiming him once silence descended upon the cabin.

He located a tablespoon, placed a paper filter in the coffeemaker's basket and measured four heaping spoons of coffee grounds into it. He filled the reservoir with tap water and hit the power button.

Crossing over to the sofa, he folded the blanket he'd used the night before, stacking it and the pillow on the side table. Soon, the scent of coffee wafted into the air. The cabin was tiny, not more than five hundred square feet. Would the smell wake Grace? Maybe he should have held off on his morning caffeine fix.

Lisa used to laugh at him and his need for coffee as soon as his feet touched the floor each morning. They'd received one of those fancy coffeemakers that made one cup of coffee at a time as a wedding gift, but he'd never gotten use to making coffee that way. He preferred to make a pot of strong, black coffee he could pour multiple cups from. No fancy-flavored creamer, either. He liked a little heavy whipping cream in his coffee, nothing else.

Lisa had eventually sold the fancy coffeemaker at a yard sale and surprised him with one that made twelve cups at a time. It was programmable, so he could prep everything the night before and awaken to the smell of fresh-brewed coffee each morning.

He smiled at the memory, and his lip quivered. That had been ten months after they married, the same day she'd told him he was going to be a father. She'd laughed and told him he'd need the extra caffeine following the sleepless nights with a newborn.

The following year was one of the happiest times in his life. Lisa had been radiant, and they had enjoyed all the milestones together—the first ultrasound, the first kick, playfully arguing over names and finally the birth.

The delivery had been difficult. After twenty-three hours of labor, Lisa's blood pressure had spiked and the doctor had to perform an emergency cesarean.

Camden had been beautiful and perfect, and Lisa had been a doting mother. Only, she had suffered from post-partum depression and had hidden it from everyone. If anyone asked how she felt, she would plaster a smile on her face and say, "Fine." When she looked tired, and he offered to hire someone to help her with the house and the baby, she'd insisted she could handle it herself. Being tired was normal when you had a newborn, she'd said.

He blamed himself for not knowing how much she was suffering. His only excuse was that he had been immersed in his job, working to achieve his goal of becoming chief of police when Chief Emerson retired. As a result he'd been unsuccessful at balancing his new family's responsibilities along with his work responsibilities.

Evan scrubbed a hand over his face. No point making excuses. He'd been a failure as a husband. He should have been more aware of his wife's feelings, insisting she seek help and ensuring she had time for herself—regular lunch dates with friends or time at the beauty salon to get her hair or nails done. Anything to give her time away from the stress of being a new mother.

Barkley whimpered, scratching at the bedroom door. "Shh, boy." Evan whispered as he hurried across the room and down the short hall to let him out. "Don't wake Grace."

The Great Dane quieted, and Evan slowly opened the door enough for the massive animal to squeeze out. A quick glance in the room showed a mound of covers in the center of the bed and a bare foot sticking out, dangling over the side. Grace was still asleep. Evan released a sigh of relief. He closed the door and tiptoed back to the kitchen.

Opening the cabinet where he'd seen dishes earlier, he found an oversize stoneware mug and poured himself a cup of coffee. Steaming mug in hand, he opened the front door and followed the Great Dane outside. There weren't any chairs on the small wooden porch, so Evan sat on the top step and watched as Barkley sniffed the perimeter of the cabin.

He took a sip of his coffee, closed his eyes and savored the moment, until his thoughts started to jumble and bump around in his brain.

They hadn't been able to locate Avery. Evan had known it was a long shot. The man wouldn't have tried to snatch Grace with so many people around if he hadn't had a planned escape route. Avery's parents insisted they hadn't seen him in four days. Evan was sure the man had gone into hiding, but he was also sure Avery wouldn't miss the unsanctioned match race today.

The only photo they'd been able to find of Avery had been a dated mug shot, one Grace said no longer provided an accurate representation of the man.

Agent Ingalls wanted Grace to attend the race to identify Avery, and Henry Green had agreed to let them have his tickets. That only left two problems. One, how could they get into the event without anyone identifying them? And two, how did he protect Grace in a crowded, open area?

Barkley ambled over to him and lay down at his feet. Evan guzzled the rest of his coffee and placed the mug on the wooden step beside him. He rested his elbows on his knees and propped his chin on his clasped hands, watching the sunrise.

Ribbons of orange and gold painted the horizon as the

morning started to awaken. The sound of the waterfall added background music to the start of the day, acting as a balm for his soul.

"Lord, I've made many mistakes in my life, the greatest of which was turning from You after we lost Lisa. My eyes are fixed on You now, and that's where they will stay. Please, help me save Grace. I can't do it without You."

TEN

The cabin was quiet. Too quiet. The only sound was the faint roar of the waterfall that had lulled Grace to sleep last night. She pulled her hair through the elastic tie, securing the ponytail. How had she slept until nine o'clock? She hadn't slept past six in ten years or longer. Why hadn't Barkley woken her? His absence from the bedroom when she woke meant only one thing. Evan must have let him out. Heat warmed her cheeks at the thought of him in her bedroom while she slept. Had she been snoring? Or drooling?

She pulled a tube of sunscreen out of her bag, squirted a small amount into her palm and applied it to her face and neck. Okay, time to find Evan and Barkley. There was no way Evan would have left her there unguarded. He had to be around somewhere. Hopefully, he'd take her back to the clinic before they had to go to the race so she could call the hospital and check on Chloe. She'd tried to call last night but didn't have cell service at the cabin.

Walking into the living area, a sleepy Barkley raised his head to look at her before curling back up in front of the fireplace. It was obvious the fire had been out for a while since there were no embers. Of course, the temperatures during the daylight hours were much warmer than the nighttime.

The smell of coffee lured her into the kitchen area. The coffeemaker was still hot, but there wasn't much left in the pot. She emptied the contents into a mug and added two spoons of sugar and a dash of cream. Her stomach rumbled, so she snagged an apple out of the basket on the counter.

The door opened before she reached it, and Bridget entered carrying a pink, hard-sided makeup bag. Evan was close behind, a small suitcase in his hand.

"Bridget, what are you doing here? Don't tell me you're my new guard." Grace smiled, hoping the other woman would know she was teasing.

"Nope. I'm here to give you a makeover. Consider me your fairy godmother." The petite redhead smiled. "Except in this case, you're not being turned into a princess, so I guess it's more of a make-under."

"Seriously?"

"Yes, seriously." Evan placed the suitcase on the floor inside the door. "Since you've agreed to attend the race— against my wishes—and to ID Avery for Agent Ingalls, we need to change your looks. We don't want Avery to ID you."

"That's where I come in." Bridget placed the makeup case on the small kitchen table and opened it. Inside was an array of lipsticks, eye shadows, creams and things. "Did you know I'm a certified makeup artist? I took a six-week course a few years ago." As she chatted away, Bridget hefted the suitcase onto the table and opened it, revealing a multitude of wigs. "A bodyguard never knows when they may need to go undercover on a job."

Evan whistled. "Wow. You really take this stuff seriously, don't you?"

"Of course I do. Sometimes it's a matter of life or death," she replied.

Grace picked up a long, straight-haired black wig. She couldn't imagine wearing such a thing. With her pale complexion and freckles, it would be obvious the hair wasn't real.

"Oh, no, that won't do for you." Bridget took the wig and laid it on a chair. She dug into the suitcase and then held up a shoulder-length, brown, curly-haired wig. "I think this one will do nicely."

She straightened and turned back to Grace. "Now, have a seat so I can get started. Getting both of you in disguises will take a couple of hours. And the match race starts at two."

"Did you figure out how you could get into the event with me?" Grace asked Evan as she sat in the hard, straight-back kitchen chair.

"Actually, I'm going to try to get away with using Henry's ticket."

"What? I thought he said the ticket wasn't transferable."

"Hold still," Bridget commanded, placing a hand under Grace's chin and lifting her face. "Close your eyes."

Grace did as instructed, acutely aware of Evan watching from across the room, a scowl on his face. "Tell me what you're thinking, Evan."

When they'd been younger, she wouldn't have had to ask what he was thinking, he would have told her or she would have instinctively known. She knew he was worried about keeping her safe, but she couldn't imagine how he planned to capture Avery.

"I don't want Henry at the race. It's too dangerous, and he's not as young as he used to be. I mean, I don't even want you there." She heard the frustration in his voice.

"But if you insist on going along with Agent Ingalls's idea, then I'm going to be at your side."

"And if the people at the gate refuse to allow you to enter?"

"Then you don't enter, either," he said flatly.

She opened her eyes, turned and frowned at him. Grace knew he was right. She couldn't risk being at the race unprotected, but she needed to do what she could to help end the threat against her family.

Bridget pulled Grace's head back into position and started applying eyeliner. Having never been one to wear much makeup, Grace was afraid to see the outcome of this makeover. Did she have the right facial wash to remove all this goop at the end of the day?

"I don't think they'll refuse me entry," Evan said.

"Why is that?"

"You've heard the old saying 'money talks'? Well, I plan to throw a little money around to see if they're listening."

"You will pretend to be married high-rollers from Texas," Bridget chimed in. "Ryan and I used a similar disguise a few months ago, only we played the part of spoiled siblings from a rich New England family."

Bridget continued to tell about her and Ryan's adventure rescuing a woman from her abusive mobster husband, but Grace tuned her out, focusing on the notion she and Evan were going to pretend to be husband and wife. There was no way that would be awkward, right?

A look of despair washed over Grace's face. Was the idea of pretending to be Evan's wife so revolting? If so, could she pull it off? Or would she blow their cover? He wished he'd had time to come up with a better plan, but it was too late to make changes now.

The air in the room suddenly became unbearably stuffy. He got up and headed to the door. "Come on, Barkley. Let's get some air."

The dog followed him outside, and Evan closed the door behind him, not waiting to see if either woman had anything to say about his sudden departure.

Why had Grace's expression made him feel rejected all over again? He wasn't an eighteen-year-old kid with idyllic dreams anymore. He was a grown man, a father, and he knew better than to allow fanciful ideas to enter his head. He and Grace would never—could never—be anything more than friends. He'd put Avery behind bars, and then, once a new veterinarian had been hired to run the clinic, Grace would return to her life in Denver. And that was fine with him. Life would go back to the way it was meant to be. He'd raise his son to the best of his ability and continue to protect the citizens of Blackberry Falls.

Well, maybe one thing would change. He thought it might be time to let Camden have the dog he'd always wanted. Seeing his son interact with Barkley had made him realize his child needed a dog that would be his best friend. A pet he could play games with and would fill the void in his heart Evan feared would be there when Grace left.

He bent, picked up a stick and tossed it. Barkley looked at the stick, but didn't budge. "Guess you don't like playing fetch, huh? Wonder if I should consider a different breed for Camden. Maybe a golden retriever or an Australian shepherd." The dog moaned and covered his face with his paw. "Okay, I didn't mean to hurt your feelings. A Great Dane would be a great choice, too."

"Great Danes are wonderful dogs, but I'd suggest you make a list of the qualities you're looking for in a pet before making a final decision." Evan startled at the sound of Grace's voice behind him. He hadn't even heard the door open.

"That's what I—" His voice faltered.

Grace's face was forever imprinted in his mind, so much so, he imagined he could draw it blindfolded. The face staring back at him was not hers. Her freckles had been replaced with high cheekbones and a beauty mark just above full, red lips. Her silver-blue eyes were now a honey-brown color, emphasized with a few wrinkles at the corners—what his mom had always called laugh lines. To top off her new look, chestnut-colored hair framed her face, falling in a cascade of curls that brushed her shoulders. If he hadn't seen it with his own eyes, he never would have believed Grace was the woman standing before him.

"Aren't you going to say anything? What do you think?" She turned, showing off the designer jeans and pink, floral-print blouse. "Will anyone recognize me?"

"Um…uh…no."

"I think he's speechless!" Bridget beamed, pushing past Grace to grab his arm. "Okay, your turn." She marched him into the cabin, pushing him onto the chair where Grace sat earlier.

"Are you going to be able to make me as unrecognizable as Grace?"

"Of course, silly. You didn't think I was going to slap a pair of fake-nose-and-mustache glasses on you and call it done, did you?" Bridget giggled. "Give me more credit than that."

"I honestly didn't know what to expect," he said, not taking his eyes off Grace. "But one thing is for sure, I'll never doubt your ability as a disguise master again."

Grace's laughter mingled with Bridget's and his heart

lifted. For the first time all day, Evan actually believed they might pull off Agent Ingalls's harebrained plan.

Evan captured Grace's hand in his own as they walked along the graveled parking area. Leaning in close, he whispered, "Stop fidgeting with your hair."

She frowned. "It's hot and itchy."

"I know. Mine is, too, but we don't want to blow our cover."

Evan honestly couldn't say whose transformation shocked him more, Grace's or his. When he'd looked into the mirror, he had truly been speechless. His ginger-colored hair had been replaced with a dark brown, short-hair wig. To complete the image, Bridget had attached facial hair with an adhesive she promised would come off with the remover she'd left behind, giving him thicker eyebrows and a close-cropped beard the same color as the wig. His appearance was so altered, he didn't think his parents or Camden would have been able to pick him out of a lineup.

Evan's gun pressed against the small of his back, offering a small amount of comfort. "Remember, let me do the talking."

She nodded. "I'll follow your lead."

They approached the guard at the gate. He had hoped Randy Ingalls would have been assigned to gate duty, guaranteeing their admittance, but he wasn't the one who greeted them. "Tickets?"

Evan handed over the tickets without saying a word. The guard, a tall, gangly ranch hand from the Hamilton ranch, glanced at the ticket, then back at Evan. "You're not Henry Green. How did you get these tickets?"

"Uncle Henry gave them to me. I'm Theodore Green the Third. Everyone calls me Trey." Evan held his breath, praying he'd disguised his voice well enough the man hadn't recognized it.

The guy looked him up and down. "I didn't know ol' Henry had a nephew."

"Actually, if you want to get technical, I'm his great-nephew. You see, he's my momma's daddy's baby brother."

"Well, *Trey*, your great-uncle Henry doesn't have the authority to give you these tickets. See right here." The man held the tickets under Evan's nose. "It says 'non-transferable.' Henry Green has to be here to use them."

"But, sir, Uncle Henry isn't coming. You might have heard, his colt, Knight's Honor, that was supposed to race today developed a bad case of colic. Anyway, Uncle Henry figured if his horse wasn't racing, there wasn't any need for him to be here. It's not like he's going to place a bet on a horse that isn't his, you know. But my wife here likes—"

"Look, Trey, I don't care what your wife likes." The man gestured to the line of people behind them. They looked annoyed. "I can't let you in. Now, kindly leave, before I have you escorted off the premises."

"I'm outta here." Grace huffed and turned on her heels, her red cowgirl boots kicking up dust. "You promised me I'd get to do some gambling on this trip. What was the point of me taking money out of the safe if I wouldn't get to have fun? I knew we should have gone to Vegas."

"What's going on here?" A big, burly man in his mid- to late-forties with thinning blond hair, wearing a tan Western suit and a Stetson hat, walked up to the gate from inside the event grounds.

"I'm sorry, Mr. Torres." The guard apologized. "These people were leaving."

Evan eyed the newcomer. The way the guard was acting, it was obvious this man was important, possibly even the person running the operation.

Putting his hand on the small of Grace's back, Evan spoke loudly. "It's okay, honey. I'll phone the pilot and tell him to get the jet fueled up and ready to go. We can be in Vegas in a few hours."

"Wait a minute." Torres motioned for them to come over to the fence, standing off to the side so others could enter. "Why don't you tell me who you are, and I'll decide if I allow you to enter or not?"

"Well, sir, like I tried to tell the man at the gate. I'm Theodore Green the Third, from Dallas. We're visiting my uncle, Henry Green, at Mountain View Ranch. Since his horse got colic—"

"Oh, good grief, Trey. Nobody cares about all that," Grace interrupted, talking in a syrupy-sweet Southern voice.

She turned to the burly man and smiled sweetly. "I'm Shelby Green." She nodded to Evan. "Trey's wife. You see, it's my birthday, which means I get to gamble. I only gamble twice a year, my birthday and New Year's Day. That way I don't get addicted, you know."

Evan bit back a smile. Grace was having fun weaving her tale, and Torres seemed to be buying it.

She got a serious look on her face, leaned in close, so only he and Torres could hear her. "What that means is my sweet man here gave me ten thousand dollars. I'm either going to gamble some, or all, of it here at your *little* horse race, or I'm headed to Vegas. The choice is yours."

"Is this a joke?"

Grace returned the man's stare, unblinking. "Oh, honey, I never joke about money."

"Cell phones must be turned off, and no cameras allowed. If you break the rules, you're outta here, and you forfeit all your bets." Torres looked to the guard and added, "Let them in."

Grace squealed and waltzed past the guard, Evan close on her heels.

Now the real test began. How many people in attendance knew Chief Evan Bradshaw and Dr. Grace Porter? Would he and Grace be able to stay in character without blowing their cover?

ELEVEN

Evan surveyed the area. A musty odor of hay, manure and horses surrounded them. The entire match race setup was crude. Horses were being held in a corral instead of a barn with stalls.

As Evan and Grace passed the holding area, a palomino colt neighed and reared on his hind legs. A handler fought to control the animal while another man stood to the side with a syringe.

When Grace's steps faltered, Evan slipped his arm around her waist and pulled her close. "Remember, don't react to anything you see."

She nodded and averted her eyes from the scene playing out in front of them, her jaw clenched.

The fact the men weren't even trying to hide what they were doing was alarming. Evan had no way of knowing what was in the syringe, but he seriously doubted it was full of vitamin supplements. He halted Grace and turned her to face him. Leaning in, he placed his lips near her cheek and whispered, "Time to take photos."

Pulling back, she met his eyes. Her lip quivered ever so slightly, but she smiled and reached up to grasp his silver-onyx bolo tie. Vanilla perfume assailed him. Her signature scent, bringing back memories of scented notes left in his locker and vanilla-lip-gloss kisses.

Mentally shaking himself, he took half a step to the right, providing a clear view for the camera hidden behind the fake stone. Grace's fingers slipped behind the oval slide, giving the appearance to onlookers she was adjusting the tie when in reality she was pressing the tiny button hidden on the back that activated the camera.

"I thought you were here to gamble." Torres walked over to them. "All you're doing is staring at your husband."

"Well, we haven't been married long, so sometimes I find myself looking at him wondering if it's real." Grace laughed. "But I'm glad you're here, Mr. . . .Torres, was it?" She paused, but the man neither confirmed nor denied his name. "Can you tell me anything about the horses racing today? So I can pick one?"

"You'll find flyers at the betting booths listing the horses and their stats." He motioned to the four booths stationed around the three-quarter-mile oval track. A man, wearing a black T-shirt with Security written across the front, walked over and whispered in his ear.

When Torres turned, his jacket flapped open, revealing a holster. "The first race starts in fifteen minutes, so place your bets," he said over his shoulder as he walked away.

Once the man was out of earshot, Grace whispered, "Did you see the gun?"

"I did, but don't focus on that." Evan squeezed her hand. "You did great. Now, we need to go to one of the booths and look at the flyers."

Her eyes widened. "We're not really going to place a bet, are we?"

"No," he assured her. "But we have to make it look like we are."

Evan took Grace's elbow and guided her toward the booth. He pulled a flyer out of the holder on the small wood shelf under the ticket window then leaned both elbows on the shelf as he pretended to study the form.

"Which horse would you like to bet on?" the woman behind the window asked.

"Not sure yet. We need to study the stats first." He pulled Grace aside and motioned for the next person in line to go ahead of them. They slowly eased away from the booth, trying not to draw attention to themselves.

Dressed in a black Security shirt, with a baseball cap pulled low to obscure his face, Agent Ingalls walked up and leaned on the metal fence railing beside them, his back to the track as he scanned the crowd.

"Don't acknowledge me. Just listen. You will find fake betting tickets stuffed inside the toilet paper roll in the last Porta Potty." He briefly made eye contact. "Nice disguises. Wouldn't have recognized you without the photo you sent earlier." And then he was gone.

Grace had clutched Evan's hand when Randy Ingalls appeared, and her nails bit into his skin. He pried his hand free. "I'm sorry," she gasped.

"It's okay." He laced his fingers through hers and smiled. "Now, let's get those tickets."

They walked to the row of Porta Potties and got in line for the one on the end. Finally, it was his turn.

"I want you to stand right outside the door," Evan said. "If you need me, yell."

"Believe me, I will." She smiled. "Loudly."

He entered the small, plastic water closet, holding his breath as he worked to quickly remove the roll of toilet paper from the holder. The tickets were exactly where Ingalls had said they would be. There were tickets for each horse in each race—smart thinking on the agent's part. This way, no matter who won the race, Evan and Grace could pretend to lose. Dividing the tickets, he slipped them into his pocket.

There was a knock on the door. "Honey. The race is about to start."

Something must have startled Grace. She wouldn't have knocked otherwise. He put the roll of paper on top of the holder and then slipped outside, taking a deep breath of fresh air.

He put his arm around her shoulders and turned her toward the track. "Everything okay?"

"I saw someone who resembled Avery's coloring and build, but I couldn't see his face."

Excitement charged through him. Avery Hebert had showed up. "Which way?"

"Over close to the corral."

Evan turned in that direction. "Well then, lets make our way over there."

They wove their way through the crowd. The first of three match races was about to start, so most of the people were vying for places to stand with the best views of the track. Evan would estimate there were close to five hundred people in attendance.

They were less than twenty feet from their destination when he saw him. But it was the person with Avery that had Evan stopping short. He looked at Grace to see if she'd noticed. Her facial expression told him she had.

"Val—"

He pulled her into his arms and claimed her lips, silencing her words. The action had been impulsive, intended to protect their cover, but in that instant, Evan knew he was in trouble. Her kiss was as sweet as he remembered, but it was an indulgence he couldn't afford.

"I'm starting to regret letting you two in here today," Torres's voice boomed behind them.

Evan pulled back, avoiding eye contact with Grace.

"A kiss for luck, that's all," Grace said, her voice husky.

Had the kiss affected her as much as it had him, Evan wondered, or was she simply embarrassed at being caught?

Whatever was the case, it didn't matter. Right now the only thing that mattered was catching Avery. Nothing else.

Grace's heart fluttered in her chest, as if it were a hummingbird searching to escape its cage. She took a few steadying breaths, willing her nerves to calm. Whatever had possessed Evan to kiss her, here of all places, in front of so many people?

She looked around, getting her bearings. Torres huffed and walked over to Avery, who now stood at the metal fence, observing the track, Valerie at his side.

Oh. Grace touched her lips, the warmth of Evan's kiss still on them. That's why he'd kissed her. She'd almost blown their cover. Shelby Green from Dallas, Texas, wouldn't know a veterinary technician from Blackberry Falls, Colorado.

"I'm sorry. I did the first thing I could think of—"

"To shut me up." She forced a smile, but her heart felt like it was sinking in quicksand. "It's okay. Let's finish what we started. I won't mess up again."

"Are you sure being here, pretending to be someone else, isn't too hard for you?" Concern laced Evan's voice.

She nodded, and he clasped her hand. "Okay, hang on tight. I don't want to lose you in this crowd."

Evan pushed through the throng, stopping to whisper something to Ingalls before nudging his way over to where Avery stood.

When the starting pistol sounded, Grace found herself standing right beside her employee. Was this woman whom she thought of as family involved in the attacks on her and Chloe?

While the crowd around them cheered, urging the two riders to the finish line, Grace observed Avery and Valerie. They laughed and cheered with the onlookers, Avery's hand on her back. Grace couldn't believe their beloved employee was mixed up with Avery and his illegal dealings. Valerie's words came back to her. *You saw the attacker's face. Can you identify him?* It all started to make sense. Though she hated to believe her friend would betray her, Grace knew Valerie would have had the opportunity and skills to falsify the medical reports.

Evan nudged her, nodding at the track. She'd been staring. Ugh. She needed to focus and not let her emotions rule her actions. If she blew their cover, it could mean their lives.

The horses were coming around the last turn, and Evan cheered beside her as if his life depended on it.

"Come on, boy! Faster!" Grace yelled, purposely omitting the horse's name.

Evan had warned her before they'd arrived not to yell out the name of a horse when cheering, because if the horse won, people would wonder why they didn't claim their "winnings." If anyone asked which horse they had placed a bet on, they'd dodge the question by replying they didn't want to jinx themselves by saying. Instead, they would wait until the race was over to announce their pick and act disappointed because they had lost.

As the horses crossed the finish line, the crowd erupted in a chorus of cheers and boos. Avery swept a giggling Valerie into a big hug. "See, darlin', I told you Freckled Charmer was a winner. Now let's go get our winnings so I can take you out for a nice dinner."

Valerie looped her arm through Avery's and said, "Let's go." The pair headed to the nearest booth, walking past Evan and Grace without recognizing them.

Whew. Grace released her breath. Bridget's disguises had worked.

Torres turned to them. "Well, how did you do, birthday girl?"

Grace frowned. "I lost."

Evan made a show of pulling the fake betting tickets out of his pocket and tearing them up. "Well, Shelby, looks like we're done here."

The burly man smirked. "Too bad. But there are still two more races. Better luck next time."

"No next time today." Grace sighed and turned to Evan. "You told me not to bet it all on the first race."

"You bet all ten thousand on the first race?" Torres questioned.

"I really thought we'd win."

The man's smirk turned to a full belly laugh. "Looks like your birthday ain't so lucky, after all." Torres walked away, headed to the betting booth.

"Let's get out of here, before he finds out we didn't place a bet."

"What about Avery and Valerie?" She twisted to look behind them. The pair had stopped to talk to Torres. Avery had a wad of money in his hand.

"The way he was talking, I have a feeling they aren't

sticking around for all the races, either." Evan steered her toward the entrance. "Even if they do, Ingalls saw him. I'm sure he's notified his partner who's stationed outside the entrance to follow them when they leave."

Grace didn't want to have gotten this close to capturing the man after her just to lose him again. Evan had warned her that no matter what they saw at the race today, he couldn't make any arrests because they were outside his jurisdiction. It was up to Agent Ingalls and his partner to determine which arrests—if any—they could make.

"What if he gives them the slip?"

Evan laughed. "There you go, trying to sound like a movie detective again."

"Ev—" She took a deep breath. "Trey. I'm serious."

"I know you are. I am, too. Your safety is my top priority."

They walked past the guard who'd tried to deny them admittance and headed for the parking area.

"Hey! Greg, stop them!" Torres yelled, running in their direction.

"Keep walking, but don't run. He may not mean us," Evan instructed her.

Darting a glance over her shoulder, Grace saw that Avery and Valerie had reached the gate. The man, Greg, stepped in front of them.

"Not them! Stop Mr. and Mrs. Texas!"

Greg spun and sprinted in their direction.

"Run!" Evan commanded.

They raced to the rental truck, a black extended-cab GMC, parked two rows over. The doors beeped as he hit the unlock button on the remote.

Greg was closing in on them when a white SUV sped out of nowhere, blocking his path. He hit the hood with his fist and yelled. The female driver laid on the horn and pulled forward as Greg tried to go around the front of her vehicle, encouraging him to yell louder while enabling them to reach the safety of the truck.

Grace climbed into the passenger seat as Evan started the engine. "Go. Go. Go!" she urged, twisting in her seat to see Greg and Torres standing in the middle of the parking lot staring after their fleeing vehicle.

Grace settled back into her seat and fastened the seat belt. "Wow, that was perfect timing the vehicle showed up when it did."

"Yes, wasn't it," he said more as a statement than a question.

"What are you not telling me?"

"Randy Ingalls's partner, Agent Katherine Lewis, was driving that vehicle." He merged onto US-50, heading toward Penrose.

"Why do you think Torres chased us?"

"I think he went to verify we placed a large bet. Found out we didn't and realized he'd been tricked."

"Could he have figured out who we were?"

"If anyone could have recognized us, it would have been Valerie. She looked straight at us when they walked by on their way to collect their winnings and didn't even blink."

"Do you think she could be the one who stole the drugs and altered the records?" Grace felt disloyal even letting the thought enter her head, but she had to ask.

"We definitely can't rule her out yet."

Grace thought of the things she'd witnessed at the race, especially the injections being given to the horses. To her knowledge, there hadn't been a veterinarian on duty like there would have been at a sanctioned race. Anger welled inside her at the thought of an employee of Porter Animal Clinic being involved in illegal activities involving animals. How could anyone who worked in a veterinary clinic take part in such an event?

Evan put his Jeep into Reverse and backed out of the space in the Denver Memorial parking deck. He hadn't planned on making the trip to Denver tonight, but after seeing Grace's disappointment over discovering Valerie with Avery, he'd wanted to do something nice for her. So, after returning the rental and retrieving his personal vehicle, he'd taken her to visit Chloe.

He glanced at Grace, sitting beside him. Though he'd only been able to remove his contacts and wig, she had erased all traces of Shelby Green before entering Chloe's hospital room. "Are you hungry? We could go through a drive-through if you'd like."

"How about we eat in Monument? There's a burger joint I like to stop at when I make this drive. It's almost halfway, and a perfect spot to stop and stretch. Plus, they make the best burgers and onion rings."

"Sounds good to me." He pulled to a stop and put tokens into the slot so the mechanical arm would rise, allowing them to exit the parking deck.

"Thank you for taking me to see Chloe tonight. I know you hadn't planned on making the trip, but I appreciate it."

"Did you enjoy your time with your sister?"

"Oh, yes. Dr. Carson seems completely satisfied with her progress." She smiled. "The swelling has gone down, and he's optimistic she'll make a full recovery."

She continued, happily rattling on, filling him in on the changes in Chloe's condition, and all the things she wanted to do with her sister once she had fully recovered. The time with her sister, even if the conversation had been one-sided, had done her good.

Evan wished he had witnessed Grace's special time with Chloe, but he'd stayed outside the room, talking to Lieutenant Johnson, who was waiting on Ryan to arrive and take over the night-shift guard duty.

"Did the doctor say when he planned to bring her out of the coma?"

"He said there's no way to know for sure. It could be tomorrow or it could be several more days." She sighed. "He promised to call me when they start the process to wake her. I really want to be there. To be the first person she sees."

"I'll do everything I can to make that happen."

"I know you will. It's the kind of person you are. You have a servant's heart, and you take care of the people in your life. That's what makes you so good at your job."

Her words jolted him. When Evan had been in high school, his main goal in everything he did had been to make Grace proud of him. She wouldn't be so proud if she knew how he'd failed Lisa. Maybe it was time to come clean.

"I'm not perfect. There have been plenty of times when I've not taken care of the people in my life. Lisa for one." His voice cracked, and he fought to tamp down the pain.

He turned onto the interstate access road and built up speed to merge onto I-225. The traffic was thick even for nine o'clock on a Sunday night.

"Do you want to talk about it?" Grace asked softly.

Did he want to? No. But he needed to tell her his secret. She had to understand so she wouldn't have too high an opinion of his abilities.

"After Lisa had Camden, she became withdrawn. She had a difficult labor. At first, I thought the trauma of the labor combined with the demands of a newborn were the reasons she seemed so tired and withdrawn. I offered to hire a nanny to help, but that infuriated her."

A pang of guilt stabbed at him for talking about his deceased wife and revealing her secrets to his first love, but he couldn't tell his story without revealing Lisa's, too.

Lord, forgive me. I'm not meaning to gossip.

A bolt of lightning lit the sky, followed immediately by a loud clap of thunder. Big, fat raindrops began to fall from the sky, obscuring his view. He turned on the wipers, but they were of little use in this downpour. Putting on the flashers, he pulled onto the shoulder of the highway.

He turned to face Grace. It was time she knew she'd made the right decision to build a life somewhere else, away from him.

"Lisa thought I was implying she wasn't capable of taking care of our son." He shook his head. "That wasn't what I meant at all."

"Of course, it wasn't," Grace insisted.

Sweet Grace, she still didn't get it. "I could have handled things better. If, instead of trying to throw money at the situation, I had paid attention and been there for my wife, I may have realized she was suffering from postpartum depression. And maybe she'd be alive today."

Grace gasped. "You don't mean she…"

"Harmed herself?" He definitely hadn't meant to imply anything like that. "No. But two weeks after we found out we were having a daughter, Lisa suffered a miscarriage and her depression deepened. She was sleeping all the time and not eating. Her appearance became very gaunt. I tried to get her to see a counselor, but she refused. Her ob-gyn prescribed a mild antidepressant, but she wouldn't take it."

Lightning danced in the night sky, and he studied it

as he tried to choose his next words. Grace sat quietly. Evan knew she would wait indefinitely for him to continue, and if he didn't, she would be okay with that, too. She'd never been pushy about needing to know everything. Even when she'd been younger, she'd seemed to instinctively know there were times people needed to keep things to themselves. It was one of the qualities he'd always admired in her.

The downpour eased enough that he could see again. So he merged back onto the interstate, driving in silence, his mind a jumble of thoughts as he waged an internal war with himself, struggling with his guilt for talking about Lisa when she wasn't there and his need to be honest. Mostly with himself, for the first time since the accident.

After he worked his way through the I-25 interchange and they were headed south, his need to be honest with Grace won. "Four months after the miscarriage, we were nearing our third wedding anniversary. I thought a change of scenery—a weekend getaway to Denver—would be good for her. For us."

Grace shifted in her seat, tucking her foot under her leg as she always did when listening intently.

"Lisa's parents had agreed to watch Camden," Evan continued. "He was twenty months old, and we'd never left him to go on a trip. I booked two nights in a nice hotel two blocks from the theater district. I had the entire trip planned, a morning of pampering in the spa for Lisa, followed by shopping, a romantic dinner and a play."

"That was thoughtful," Grace said.

Unfortunately, Lisa hadn't seen it that way. She'd accused him of being controlling and said he shouldn't have planned such a trip without checking with her first. It hadn't mattered what he'd said, she'd been looking for a fight. His second biggest regret from that weekend, besides planning it in the first place, was that he hadn't taken her straight back to Blackberry Falls when she'd first complained.

The exit for Monument came into view.

"Where's the burger joint?" he asked.

She directed him to a small all-night diner.

There were half a dozen cars in the parking lot. He pulled into an empty space about twenty feet from the door. The rain had become a torrential downfall. They were going to get soaked. Evan opened the center console, pulled out a blue compact umbrella and held it out to her. "Here. You use this."

She accepted the offering but didn't move. "What happened that weekend?"

Grace was waiting for him to finish telling her about Lisa. Hmm. Maybe she had changed when it came to fulfilling her curiosity. Oh, well. Since he was the one who had brought up the topic and insisted on baring his soul, he'd finish.

"She hated the entire trip and refused to leave the room." A clap of thunder shook the vehicle. "I finally convinced her to go to dinner and the play…it was one she'd wanted to see for a while. I promised her if she'd do that much, we'd cut our trip short. After the play, we'd go straight back to the hotel, check out and head home, but—" His voice cracked. "We never made it back to the hotel."

Grace reached across the seat and clasped his hand. Her touch burned like a brand.

"I'm sorry. I heard about the drive-by shooting. I didn't know it was an anniversary trip, or that Lisa had suffered from postpartum."

"It wasn't something we announced." Evan pulled his

hand free of her grasp, opened his door and ran for the awning covering the diner's door, ignoring the rain pelting his body.

He didn't want Grace's pity. He simply needed her to understand she'd made the right choice in walking away. And she needed to remember that, since he could never give his heart away again. Not to anyone. Even her.

TWELVE

Evan had just run through the rain to the diner, away from her. Shame washed over Grace. She hadn't meant to seem insensitive with her comment. Of course, they hadn't announced Lisa's postpartum depression, but it was Blackberry Falls where everyone knew everything. She was impressed he'd been able to keep it a secret.

But why had he told her? Had being in Denver twice in the past few days brought all the memories crashing down on him? His pain was evident, and it made her heart ache.

She'd been happy Evan had found someone to spend his life with, and she hated that he and Camden had to live without Lisa in their lives any longer. Grace owed him an apology. Whether or not he'd accept it, she didn't know, but she'd have to try.

The rain beat against the windows. She looked at the compact umbrella. Even if it could offer enough protection from the downpour, once she opened the door and stuck the umbrella out to open it, she'd be soaking wet.

Tossing the umbrella back into the center console, Grace plucked her oversize leather messenger bag off the floorboard, opened her door and dashed across the parking lot to Evan's side.

"Why didn't you use the umbrella?"

She shrugged. "The way the rain is blowing, I didn't think an umbrella would do much good." Tugging the door open, she added, "Come on, I'm starved."

The moment she entered the diner, the smell of greasy burgers and salty fries assaulted her. The interior of the restaurant was a nod to a fifties diner without coming off as a cheesy imitation. The floors were black-and-white vinyl tiles laid in a checkerboard pattern. The tables were red Formica, and the booth seats were covered in red-and-white vinyl. That was where the similarity ended.

Instead of a jukebox full of rock 'n' roll songs, country music played through surround-sound speakers, and instead of a dress with an apron, the waitress wore blue jeans and a red, polo-style shirt.

Grace slid into a booth next to the front window and pulled out a laminated menu, even though she knew exactly what she would order. It kept her hands busy.

Evan slid into the seat across from her. "This place is…interesting."

"Kind of old meets new, wouldn't you say?"

"Exactly." He rubbed his hand over his fake beard. "You know, I'm regretting we didn't bring a change of clothes."

She smiled. "It sure was funny seeing Lieutenant Johnson's face when he finally realized we were telling the truth about who we were."

"He didn't believe it until we took out our contacts and pulled off the wigs." He scratched at the beard again. "This thing is itching. I wish I'd brought the adhesive dissolvent."

"Oh. Why didn't I think of this sooner? I might have something that would work." She dug into her purse and took out a small blue makeup bag with a hummingbird-print design. Unzipping the bag, she pulled out a rect-angular tin, a small plastic bottle and an individually wrapped nail polish remover pad.

Evan leaned over the table for a better view. "What is all this stuff?"

She held up the tin. "Cotton swabs." Then she picked up the bottle. "Baby oil."

He reached across and picked up the small pink square packet. "An acetone nail polish remover pad?"

"That is a last resort," she laughed, handing him the supplies. "I'm pretty sure, if you apply the baby oil and wait a minute or two, the adhesive will break down and you'll be able to remove the beard. You already took off the wig, and not to be mean or anything, you kinda look funny with red hair and a dark brown beard and eyebrows."

He pointed to his face and wiggled his eyebrows. "Re-ally? You think this looks funny."

Grace choked back laughter as the waitress walked up to their table and set down two glasses of water.

"Hi, my name is Kenzie. I'll be taking your order. What can I get you to drink?" The woman looked like she should be performing with a rock band instead of working in a diner. In her early twenties, she had short black hair, several piercings, including a nose ring, and an intricate dogwood-flowers tattoo covering most of her right arm.

Evan motioned for Grace to go first.

"I'd like coffee, please. And if you don't mind, could we go ahead and place our food order, too?"

"Sure, no problem," Kenzie replied.

"Great, I'd like a cheeseburger, all the way, and an order of onion rings," she said, putting the unopened menu back in its table holder.

The girl wrote everything on her order pad. Then she turned to Evan. "And for you, sir?"

"I'll have the same."

"Okay. I'll be right back with your coffee." She took a few steps then stopped and turned back to Evan. "You know, if you're going to wear a fake beard and mustache, you should get a good quality one that matches your natural hair."

Grace exploded in laughter as Kenzie walked away.

Evan held up both hands, palms forward in mock surrender. "Okay. Okay. I'll go take off the facial hair. I'm tired of itching." He slid out of the booth and then removed the bolo tie. Slipping it into his inside jacket pocket, he removed the jacket and folded it before holding it out to her. "Do you mind hanging on to this while I'm gone?"

"No problem." She accepted the jacket, placing it under her purse beside her on the seat.

Evan held up his phone. "I'll be as quick as possible, but if anything happens, call."

She nodded, and he headed to the restroom at the back of the diner.

Kenzie brought two large mugs of coffee to the table along with a red-plastic food basket full of small tubs of individual servings of cream. As she took the items off the tray and placed them on the table, a small wolf tattoo on her inner wrist triggered a flash memory—of a different wolf tattoo on the forearm of the intruder who'd attacked Grace two nights earlier in the clinic.

Grace's breath caught, and the girl looked at her quizzically.

"Sorry. Your, um, wolf tattoo reminded me of someone."

After the girl walked away, Grace emptied the contents of two tubs of creamer into her cup and stirred. Lifting the mug with shaking hands, she took a sip, willing the coffee's warmth to chase away the sudden chill in the air and, hopefully, to evaporate the stress of this very trying day.

Her gaze drifted to the parking lot. The rain had slowed to a drizzle. With any luck, it would stop before they left the diner.

A vehicle pulled into the lot, and she watched as Mr. Torres and Greg the guard got out. What were they doing here?

Grace's heart slammed against her chest. With a trembling hand, she placed the mug on the table, creamy, brown liquid sloshing out. Pulling three or four napkins from the silver dispenser on the table, she mopped up the spill.

What should she do? Would they recognize her? The only thing to give her away was her clothes. Think fast. Opening her messenger bag, she pulled out a lightweight beige sweater she'd stuffed inside on a whim when leaving the cabin earlier. She quickly pushed her arms though the sweater's sleeves and buttoned it all the way to the top. She then tucked the collar of her pink-floral blouse inside so the fabric wouldn't show.

Slipping her phone out of her purse, she started to call Evan, but hesitated for fear of being overheard. She quickly sent him a text instead. Torres and Greg are here.

The bell over the door sounded as the men entered the diner. They looked around and then headed in her direction. Glancing down, she closed the text screen, pulled up a word game and pretended to be absorbed in her phone.

"Well, well, well, if it ain't Dr. Porter. What are you doing so far from Blackberry Falls?" The two men slipped into the booth, uninvited, and sat across from her.

Torres snapped his fingers. "Oh, right. I heard about the attack on your sister. I guess you've been to visit her. How's she doing?"

Do not register a reaction. Remember, you've never met them before. Don't act like you know them.

Grace looked at the man and tilted her head. "I'm sorry? Have we met?"

"I guess not. Let me introduce myself." He smiled and held out his hand "My name is Antonio Torres."

She ignored his offer of a handshake, and Greg snickered. Torres shot his goon a look, and the man choked down the laugh.

Dropping his elbows on the table, Torres clasped his hands together and rested his chin on top of them. "I truly was sorry to hear about Dr. Osborne's wife. Do they know who attacked her? Is she going to be okay?"

Where was Evan?

She glanced toward the back of the diner. The men's room door opened, and he stepped out, looking like his old self. He still sported the white dress shirt and the suit pants he'd worn to the race, but without the bolo and the jacket, he didn't resemble his alter ego Trey. Evan met her gaze and winked. Relief surged through her.

Turning back to Torres she replied, "Thank you for your concern, but I'd rather not discuss my personal business."

Torres leaned back, a look of shock on his face. "No need to get defensive. I was only being neighborly."

"Excuse me, but you're in my seat," Evan said, stopping to stand beside her.

"Chief Bradshaw. I didn't know you were here, too," Torres said, not moving.

"Now you do. Like I said, you're in my seat, Mr. Torres."

The man raised an eyebrow, shock evident on his face.

"Don't look so surprised. I always make it a habit to know newcomers to the area."

Torres jerked his head for Greg to get up and then slid out of the booth behind him. Evan slid into the vacated spot, reached across the table and took her hand.

At his touch, a jolt of awareness shook her. Had Evan felt it, too? His thumb massaged the back of her hand, and the anxiety she'd felt when Torres and Greg entered the diner evaporated.

Grace plastered on a smile and looked up at Antonio Torres, who stood, seemingly rooted to the spot, staring at them. "If you'll excuse us, it looks like our waitress is headed this way with our food."

"Sure," he said, looking from her to Evan. "Enjoy your meal."

After he'd walked away, Evan gave her hand a gentle squeeze, his smile warming her in a way coffee never could.

The waitress delivered their meal. Suddenly the thought of eating the greasy food she had craved made Grace feel nauseous. She wondered if she'd be able to swallow even one bite with the two men sitting a few booths away.

Torres and Greg sat in the corner booth two tables away. Far enough away to look like they were leaving Evan and Grace alone, but close enough to overhear each other's conversation. At least they had sat where Evan had a clear view of them and Grace didn't, though he doubted she'd forget the men were near.

"Let's give thanks." Evan leaned in close, still holding Grace's hand tightly in his, and prayed.

"Amen," she echoed as he finished, offering him a lopsided smile.

Suddenly he wanted nothing more than to load her, Camden and Barkley into his vehicle and get far away from the danger lurking around her.

"Thank you," she said as she pulled her hand free. "Living alone, it's been a while since I've had someone else to pray over a meal for me."

"My pleasure," he replied, swallowing the sorrow rising within him at the thought of all the meals they could have shared if things had been different. Only, if things had been different, he wouldn't have Camden, and he could never imagine his life without his son. Though he'd forever regret failing her when she'd needed him most, he'd never regret loving Lisa.

Shaking the cobwebs of memory from his mind, he poured a blob of ketchup onto his plate and dipped an onion ring into the condiment before taking a bite and forcing the food past the lump in his throat. "Yu-um You were right. These are delicious."

Grace looked as if she needed to tell him something, but he sensed this wasn't the time or place. "Later," he whispered and nodded to her plate. "Eat."

She picked up her burger, took a bite, chewed and swallowed. Then she smiled and took a bigger bite. Good. He'd been afraid Grace's rattled nerves wouldn't allow her to eat, and she hadn't eaten much the past few days, her already slim frame starting to look gaunt.

When both of their plates were empty, Evan motioned to the waitress to bring their check. Food had just been delivered to Torres's table, and though Evan had no way of knowing if the man was a threat to Grace, he'd feel better getting out of the area ahead of him and his goon.

Kenzie brought their bill, and he handed her more

than enough cash to cover the total plus leave her with a generous tip.

In the meantime, Grace rolled his jacket into a tight ball and stuffed it into her purse. He'd wondered why she'd carried such a large bag, now he knew. It was so she could hide things in it.

They stepped out into the cool night air. The rain had stopped, leaving a sweet, fresh scent in its wake.

Evan guided Grace to his Jeep, opening the passenger-side door for her. "I couldn't say it earlier—too many listening ears—but you did great in there. Actually, you've been great all day, the way you slipped into character as Shelby and all."

She laughed. "I guess watching those whodunit movies paid off."

"I guess so," he smiled and closed the door.

Rounding the vehicle, he quickly slid behind the wheel and started the engine. Evan cast one last glance at the diner and his smile evaporated, the hairs on the nape of his neck tingling. Torres was staring in his direction, a cell phone to his ear.

Putting the vehicle in Reverse, he exited the parking lot. Time to get Grace back to the safety of the cabin.

"You missed the on-ramp," Grace noted as he sped past the interstate and turned right onto 2nd Street.

"I know. I think we'll stick to back roads tonight."

"You think they'll follow us, don't you?"

"I'm not sure. But they'll expect us to take the interstate, so the back roads should be safer."

"When you say 'back roads,' you don't mean an off-road trail as in the dirt-and-gravel road that goes over the mountain, do you?"

Was Evan imagining the sound of fear in her voice?

Had his honesty about how he'd failed Lisa caused Grace to doubt his ability to protect her?

"Yes. But I'll also call Agent Ingalls and make him aware of the situation." He gave her a reassuring smile. "It's going to be okay. I promise."

"Do you realize how many times you've said 'I promise' to me in the past three days?"

Had he said it a lot? He had no idea. "I take it I've said it several times. Doesn't mean I'm any less sincere."

"I know. You wouldn't make a promise unless you meant to keep it, but don't make promises that are out of your control. Whether or not everything is okay isn't up to you." Her voice softened. "All you can do is try to make the best choices in any given situation and know the rest is in God's hands."

Evan processed her words as he turned onto Mt. Herman Road—as Grace had said, a dirt-and-gravel road. A trail favorite of mountain bikers, it wasn't ideal for automobile travel, especially on a dark and stormy night. Nonetheless, it would help carry them across the mountain where, after several turns, they'd follow County Road 11 south to Blackberry Falls, adding an extra hour of travel.

Grace shifted in her seat and stared at him, waiting for a reply. She was right. No matter the outcome, God was in control.

"Pray more, worry less. That's what my mom always said to me when I was growing up. Okay, I won't make promises of things I have no power over." He swallowed. Why had it taken him so long to learn that lesson? He'd made promises to Lisa the last night of her life, but he hadn't been able to fulfill them.

"I'm not worried. I trust you," she replied.

He pressed the voice command on the steering wheel

to put a call into Agent Ingalls, but the call wouldn't go through. No cell signal. Why hadn't he tried before turning onto the rutted-out old dirt road?

Dear Lord, it's too late to change the route now. I pray I made the right choice. Please, keep us safe.

The road was narrow, and on a good day, when the sun was shining, it took about an hour to drive across. Unfortunately, today wasn't a good day. It was a dark, moonless night, and the road was muddy.

"It seemed like there was something you wanted to tell me back at the diner. What was it?" he asked Grace.

"Oh, yeah." She turned in her seat to look at him as she often did when talking. "Kenzie, our waitress, had a wolf tattoo. When I saw it, I remembered the guy who attacked me at the clinic had one."

"Identical to hers?"

"No. His was a wolf's head inside a triangle, on the inside of his forearm. I'm sorry I didn't remember it sooner."

"No need to be sorry. Memories can't be forced, sometimes they have to happen organically."

"I guess. Do you think it will help us catch the guy?"

"Possibly. When we get back to the cabin, I'll have you draw a rough sketch of what you saw. Then I can send it out to the tattoo parlors in the area to see if anyone remembers doing the work."

Evan rounded a bend a little too fast and the Jeep fishtailed, the nose coming to a stop too close to the edge of the road and a steep drop.

"Well, that was like a ride at a theme park, only not as much fun." Grace laughed nervously.

"I underestimated how slick this road would be after the heavy rainfall. Sorry," he replied as he shifted the vehicle into four-wheel drive. He needed to put as many miles between them and Torres as possible, but he couldn't be careless in the process.

They continued the ride in silence. Evan drove slow and steady, his nerves tautening with each passing mile. If Grace was nervous, she didn't say anything. Maybe she was afraid of distracting him while they were on this road.

They finally reached the other side of the mountain, and it had only taken them twenty minutes longer than normal.

Being back in cell service range, Evan tried to reach Randy Ingalls again, but the call went to voice mail. He left a message, asking the agent to call, and then he turned onto County Road 11, headed south toward Blackberry Falls. They would arrive at the cabin in forty-five minutes, a little before midnight.

"Do you think Torres being at the diner was a coincidence?" Grace asked the question he'd been pondering ever since he'd received her text while removing Trey Green's persona in the men's room.

Touching the tips of his fingers to his brow line, Evan was reassured to know he did, indeed, still have eyebrows. The beard and mustache had been removed using the nail polish remover, but when Grace's text arrived, he'd been struggling to get the fake eyebrows off. In the end, he'd pulled them off in one quick, painful tug.

"I've been thinking about that." He sighed. "Unless they followed us from the hospital, I can't imagine them knowing we were at the diner. I took every precaution and didn't see anyone tailing us. And I don't believe Torres would have left the match race until all the races were over and all the money counted, which would have given us at least a two-hour head start."

"So, you're saying it was a coincidence?"

"Yes, but that doesn't mean Torres isn't a threat. The fact he made a point of talking to you concerns me."

"Yeah, it concerned me, too." Grace pulled her sweater tighter.

Evan didn't know if she was chilled from the cool night or if it was nerves. He reached over and turned up the heat, adjusting the vents so the air would warm her.

A truck came speeding up behind them. He couldn't be sure because they were out in the country and there weren't any streetlights, but it looked a lot like the truck that had tried to push them into the oncoming train the night Chloe had been attacked. Evan sped up. He had to lose them before they reached the turnoff to the cabin.

Grace twisted in her seat to look out the rear window, but didn't say a word.

Evan's phone rang. He hit the answer button on the steering wheel. "Chief Bradshaw here."

"We lost Avery Hebert." Agent Ingalls's voice sounded over the speaker.

Evan glanced at Grace, her eyes still focused on the vehicle tailing them. "I think we found him."

"Where are you?" Ingalls asked.

"County Road 11. About fifteen miles north of the Flying V Ranch."

Grace screamed, "He's going to hit us!" She twisted around in her seat, facing the front as the truck rammed into the back of Evan's vehicle. Metal crunched against metal, and his tires skidded on the wet pavement.

"Bradshaw, what's happening?" Ingalls asked urgently.

"He's trying to make us crash." Tightening his grip on the steering wheel, Evan spared a brief glance at Grace. "Are you okay?"

"I'm fine. But how are we going to stop him?" She

looked over her shoulder and then back to him again. "Can I hold the steering wheel, and you shoot his tires or something?"

"Don't do anything reckless," Ingalls yelled across the speakers. "We've notified the sheriff's office, and I'm on my way." The call went silent.

Evan sped up, putting a little distance between him and the truck, but the other driver soon closed the gap, ramming into them again. This time the impact shattered the back window, but Evan had been able to hold the Jeep steady without skidding.

Evan raced away again, driving dangerously fast on the wet road. His headlights flashed on a bright yellow diamond-shaped road sign, and an eerie, sinking feeling settled in the pit of his stomach. A quick glance in the rearview mirror showed the truck was still barreling down on them—and they were fast approaching the Hangman's Noose curve.

His analytical brain immediately pulled up the stats. No less than ten accidents occurred on that curve per year and, on average, two fatalities annually. It was little surprise they hadn't passed one vehicle since ending up on this stretch of road, most of the locals knew to avoid this area at night, especially following a thunderstorm when the road would be slick.

Evan could only see one option if he hoped to avoid crashing in the curve. Thankfully, there wasn't any oncoming traffic. "Looks like we will have to try a stunt-man maneuver from one of your whodunit shows. Hold on tight."

Grace gripped the armrest and prayed in a muffled whisper.

Evan inhaled. Took his foot off the gas and allowed the other vehicle to almost kiss his bumper. Tightening his grip on the steering wheel, he darted into the other lane. And slammed on his brakes. The truck came alongside him. The other driver swerved into them, clipping the front of the Jeep. Metal clashing with metal, sparks flying like fireflies. Evan struggled to control the spin. His vehicle did doughnuts on the pavement then slid off the road, sideswiping a tree before landing with the rear wheels wedged in the ditch. Thankfully, the impact wasn't hard enough for the airbags to deploy.

"Are you hurt?" he asked Grace.

"I don't think so," she replied.

Evan tried to push open his door. Stuck. He twisted enough to get a booted foot against the door and kicked, hard. After the third try, the door popped open. "Call nine-one-one. Tell them there's been an accident."

"Where are you going?" she asked, fear evident in her voice.

"I've got to check on the other vehicle. I'm pretty sure it was Avery driving. But I was so focused on trying to keep us alive that I didn't see if he got away or if he crashed, too." He took her hand in his. "Are you sure you're okay?"

"Yes. Just a little shaken."

He put his hand on the side of her head. Burying his fingers in her hair, he leaned in and claimed her lips. Not a kiss to stop her from talking, like the one earlier that afternoon, but a kiss of need. One to satisfy his mind that she was okay. That he was okay. And they would get through this. His heart soared, a new energy running through his veins. He felt a heightened sense of awareness, like he had been asleep and had just awakened and could accomplish anything. Right now he needed to conquer their attacker.

Reluctantly pulling back, his eyes connected with

hers. "Stay here. If the doors will lock, lock them. Don't open them until I get back. I'll be as quick as I can."

She nodded, searching his face in silent assessment. He didn't regret the kiss—he had needed it at that moment, as surely as his body needed oxygen to live, though he knew he'd have to answer for it later.

Opening the console, he took out his Glock and a flashlight, stepped out of the vehicle and closed the door. Time to make sure Avery wasn't circling back around to attack again.

THIRTEEN

The clouds parted, allowing the full, bright moon to shine through, providing a minimal amount of light. Evan scrambled up the bank. When he reached the pavement, he clicked on the flashlight, sweeping the beam in an arc from one side of the road to the other. Black tire marks on the asphalt showed the location where his vehicle had spun and skidded. Approximately fifty feet away, a series of yellow road signs with black arrows marked the start of the curve. They had barely escaped the Hangman's Noose.

The low hum of an idling engine drew his attention. He picked up the pace, running down the incline of the curve, one hand holding the flashlight and the other hovering near his gun.

The flashlight beam illuminated a man in the ditch, lying stomach-down, his face turned heavenward. Evan squatted beside him. No pulse. Avery Hebert was dead; his neck had been broken.

The truck had come to rest against a big oak tree roughly ten yards away from the victim, the driver's door hung open. Evan crossed to it, reached in and turned the engine off. Avery must not have been wearing his seat belt.

Evan needed to call for the coroner. He reached in his back pocket for his phone. It wasn't there. Ugh. Frustration soared through him as he started walking back to the spot where his vehicle sat in a ditch, the steep slope of the curve making going up much more difficult than coming down had been.

Evan had wanted to stop Avery from killing him and Grace, but he hadn't wanted the man dead. He had needed answers from Avery, namely had he acted alone or had he been working for someone.

Was Grace safe now that Avery was dead, or was she in greater danger from an unknown threat?

Grace may have been cold earlier, but not anymore. The inside of the SUV was stifling. Her heart raced and sweat beaded on her forehead. She'd love nothing more than to step outside the vehicle and allow the night air to cool her, but she dared not get out until Evan returned.

Every event of the day had seemed more escalated than the previous one. To top it off, she had no idea how to interpret Evan's kiss. He'd kissed her at the match race because she'd been about to blow their cover, but why had he kissed her just now like a warrior going off to battle?

And what a kiss it had been. Grace hadn't been kissed like that in…well…fifteen years. Evan had always been the only man who could churn up her emotions like that. Lifting her hair off her neck, she fanned herself with her free hand.

What was taking Evan so long? Had Avery crashed in the curve and been injured? She couldn't imagine Avery escaping unscathed driving at such a high speed on a wet road. He had to have known he was putting himself at risk, not only her.

A shudder ran the length of her body. He hadn't only

targeted her, but Avery would have killed Evan, too, leaving Camden an orphan.

Sirens pierced the silence, pulling Grace from her thoughts. Help had arrived. She craned her neck as red, blue and yellow lights strobed across the front windshield. Car doors slammed, and she heard the pounding of feet headed in her direction. There was a rap on the driver's-side window.

"Ma'am. Are you okay?" A man, shrouded in darkness, peered inside.

She reached forward and then paused, her hand hovering over the handle. Evan had made her promise not to exit the vehicle until he returned. She thought the man on the other side of the door was a police officer, but she couldn't make out his uniform or his badge.

A beam of light bounced along the windshield as the man went around the vehicle to her side. He rattled the door handle. "Ma'am. Open the door."

She shook her head. He took a step back, his eyes never leaving hers. He must think she'd addled her brain in the accident.

He touched his shoulder, and she heard the static sound of a radio. "Where's the ambulance?"

After a moment of silence, the dispatcher replied, "ETA three minutes. Are you able to assess the injuries?"

"Negative. There's a female victim. Age thirty, thirty-five. She doesn't appear to be injured, but she refuses to exit the vehicle. Do the responding EMTs know sign language?"

Grace fought to suppress the hysterical giggle tickling the back of her throat. The man *was* a sheriff's deputy. She couldn't have him thinking she was deaf.

Opening the door, she slid out of the Jeep. Surely,

Evan wouldn't be upset with her for getting out since a police officer was here.

"I'm sorry, Officer—" she leaned close to read his badge "—Rice." Seeing his surprised expression, she quickly added, "No, I'm not deaf… I guess I was still stunned from the accident."

"Understandable." The officer grasped her elbow and steadied her. "What's your name, ma'am?"

"Grace Porter."

"Are you hurt anywhere, Ms. Porter?"

She shook her head.

"Was someone else with you? Who was driving?"

"Police Chief Evan Bradshaw. He went to check on the driver of the other vehicle."

"Okay." Officer Rice nodded as he guided her up the slight incline of the ditch. "My partner went to check out the curve, so they should see each other."

They reached the top of the embankment, and Evan raced toward them. He immediately pulled out his wallet and displayed his badge. "Officer Hooper is putting out flares. I don't expect we'll see much traffic, but we'll need another officer to help direct just in case." He paused and flicked a glance at her before turning back to Officer Rice. "We'll also need the coroner. There's one fatality in the curve."

She gasped. "Is it Avery?"

Evan nodded.

The man who had injured Chloe and tormented Grace was dead? Bile rose in her throat and a wave of dizziness assaulted her.

Evan put a hand on her lower back and led her to a boulder on the side of the road. "Sit here until the ambulance arrives." He knelt beside her, holding his flashlight off to the side where it would cast a glow across her face. "Are you okay? Did you hit your head when we wrecked?"

"No. And I don't have a concussion."

Officer Rice stood a few feet away talking to Dispatch.

Evan lifted her chin and searched her eyes. She knew he was looking to see if her pupils were dilated.

"I'm fine," she whispered. "Is Avery really dead?"

"Yes."

"Does this mean it's over? My sister and I can live our lives in peace?" She felt like a horrible person because her first thought was of her and her sister's safety and not of the sadness Avery's family would endure at his loss.

He shrugged. "I don't know."

Grace wanted to ask what he knew, but she swallowed the question. Evan had always been honest with her. If he had more information, he'd tell her. Hounding him wouldn't help.

An ambulance arrived on the scene, followed close behind by a large, black SUV with tinted windows.

Randy Ingalls stepped out of the SUV and headed their way. "Are you both okay?"

"We're fine." Evan stood and turned toward the agent. "Avery Hebert is dead. He crashed in the curve."

The EMT pushed his way past Evan and Ingalls and came to her side. "Do you hurt anywhere, Dr. Porter?"

"I'm fine," she answered, looking at the man's badge. Patterson. "You're one of the first responders who helped my sister the other night."

"Yes, ma'am." He held up a penlight and checked her pupils. "Can you walk?"

"Yes." She sighed. "I really am fine. I was wearing my seat belt. My shoulder will be sore and bruised in the morning. Other than that, I don't have any injuries."

Patterson smiled. "Good. I'm glad you had on your

seat belt. Now, let's walk over to the ambulance. I'll check your blood pressure and oxygen levels and make sure you really are fine."

Standing to the side talking to Randy Ingalls, Evan gave her a stern look and jerked his head toward the ambulance. He then turned his attention back to the agent. If his and the agent's animated discussion was an indicator, Evan would be tied up awhile.

She was tired. All she wanted was to go home—or back to the cabin—make sure Barkley was okay, and go to sleep. Reluctantly, she allowed Patterson to help her to her feet and guide her to the ambulance. Maybe, if she permitted the EMTs to check her out, she could convince Evan to have one of the officers drive her to the Vincents' cabin.

Evan lifted the cup to his mouth and drained it. The coffee was strong and bitter, but he needed the caffeine boost before making the drive from the station to the cabin. He'd never intended to be away from Grace for this long, but it had been a long night. First, he'd had to complete the paperwork. Then, he'd had to go out to Ralph and Lydia Hebert's home to tell them their son was dead. As a parent himself, that was always one of the hardest parts of his job; no parent should ever have to bury their child. No matter what evil things Avery had done, his parents loved him.

He placed the mug on his desk and stood. Time to go to the cabin and see Grace. He needed to let her know they hadn't been able to confirm whether Avery was working with someone or alone. Valerie had been brought in for questioning, but she had seemed genuinely shocked that Avery had been the man who'd attacked Chloe and tried to kill Grace. She insisted she and Avery hadn't been dating long. As a matter of fact, the match race had only been their second date. Evan had no evidence to tie her to the attacks, and in his gut, he believed she was innocent.

Lifting a hand in farewell to Lieutenant Johnson, Evan stepped out of the station. The sun had begun to rise, casting the morning in a beautiful golden light. The beauty of the day brought joy to his heart, and he was suddenly in a great hurry to get to Grace.

A woman of medium height with shoulder-length black hair and unnaturally violet eyes blocked his path. Marcia O'Neal. What could have brought her to the station so early in the morning?

All of his senses instantly went on high alert. "Can I help you?"

"Chief Bradshaw, I…" She swallowed and then blurted, "James Osborne is behind the attack on Chloe."

Evan's pulse quickened. Did James's mistress hold the evidence they had been searching for?

"Let's step inside and talk." He retraced his steps, holding the door open for her to precede him inside. Upon entering the building, he motioned to Johnson to follow them into his office.

Once the door was closed and Evan was seated at his desk with Marcia in the faux-leather guest chair facing him and Johnson standing to the side, Evan turned to Marcia. "Ms. O'Neal, would you mind repeating what you said outside?"

She looked at Johnson and said, "I have reason to believe James Osborne is behind the attack on Chloe."

Lieutenant Johnson leaned on the corner of the desk. "What led you to that conclusion?"

Marcia pulled a tissue out of the box on the desk. "I'm sure you've heard James and I, um, that we…"

"Have been dating?" Evan asked softly.

She nodded, absently shredding the tissue in her hands. "I'm not a home-wrecker you know. James told me the marriage was over. He moved out and was working toward getting his divorce."

"Marcia, what evidence do you have James is behind the attacks?" Evan was tired and didn't have the patience needed to sit and listen to her rationale for taking up with a married man.

"I overheard a phone conversation last night." She took a deep breath, her eyes focused on destroying the tissue.

"I'm curious." He leaned forward, his elbows on his desk. "Why would James have such a conversation in your presence?"

Marcia met his gaze, unwavering. "He didn't know I was there. I thought I'd surprise him with a home-cooked meal. I made a lasagna." She looked back down at her hands, the tissue nothing more than confetti now. "When I went up the steps to the porch, I heard him on the phone. The windows were open. I peeked in the window to his office, thinking I'd get his attention so he could let me in, then I could go into the kitchen and set the meal up."

"But?" Johnson prompted. His focus zeroed in on the young woman, and Evan knew his lieutenant was reading her body language.

"James sounded furious. I heard him tell the person on the other end of the line they better not mess up the job like they bungled the last one." Marcia looked from Evan to Johnson and back again. "I don't know what *job* he was talking about."

"It's okay. I do." Evan's gut tightened. Instinct told him James had been talking to Avery, and the job had been to kill him and Grace. "Did you hear anything else?"

"He told the person if they had…" Marcia shuddered

and tears started streaming down her face. "Had…killed Chloe like they were paid to do, there wouldn't be a mess to clean up now."

Evan met Johnson's eyes. His lieutenant inclined his head in a subtle nod. He believed Marcia was telling the truth. So did Evan.

Reaching for his desk phone, Evan buzzed Reba Franklin and ordered the dispatcher to send an officer to pick up Dr. James Osborne and bring him in for questioning.

Johnson put a hand on Marcia's shoulder. "Is there any way James could know you overheard his conversation?"

She shook her head. "I left without him seeing me."

There was one more detail Evan had to know. "You said this was last night?"

"Yes. Around six o'clock."

Over five hours before he and Grace had landed in the ditch and Avery had been killed. He bit back an exclamation and took a deep breath, releasing it slowly. "May I ask why it took you twelve hours to report this?"

"I was in shock. I thought maybe I'd misheard the conversation." Her eyes pleaded with him to understand. "I couldn't reconcile that the man I knew would be capable of something like this."

"What changed your mind?"

"I heard about what happened last night. You and Dr. Porter. And Avery." Her voice cracked. "I got to thinking about how Dr. Porter was the one who saved her sister from the intruder, and it made me wonder if she was the *mess* James wanted *cleaned up*."

Marcia wailed, "It's my fault. A man's dead. And you and Dr. Porter could have been hurt." She jumped out of her seat, the shredded tissue tumbling off her lap and onto the floor like snow. "I'm sorry I didn't come in last night. I wasn't trying to obstruct justice."

"It's okay. You came in. That's the important thing," Lieutenant Johnson said, pulling additional tissues from the box and pressing them into her hand.

Marcia settled back onto the chair, wiping her face and sniffling.

The phone on Evan's desk buzzed, and he picked up the receiver. "Yes?"

"Sir, we haven't been able to locate Dr. Osborne. He isn't at his house or the clinic."

"Okay, put an APB out on his vehicle. A black Por—"

"Excuse me, Chief Bradshaw," Marcia interrupted. "James told me he had to take his vehicle in for service Saturday afternoon and it would be in the shop for a few days."

"Do you know what he's driving in the meantime?"

"I know he got a rental. Last night, I noticed there was a white sedan in the drive. But I don't know the make or model. I'm sorry." She appeared deeply concerned she couldn't provide additional information.

"It's okay. You've given us a lot of important information." He reached out his hand. "Thank you for coming in."

Turning to his lieutenant, he added, "Take Ms. O'Neal to your office and write up her statement, then see she gets home safely."

Speaking into the phone, he relayed the new information and instructed Reba to have an officer check out the rental car places and dealerships within a thirty mile radius.

Time to get to the cabin and ensure Grace stayed safe. He exited the building at an almost full-on sprint, thankful he'd had enough sense to have an officer pick up his police SUV from his home and deliver it to the station after the accident last night.

Lord, please don't let James get to her. I just got her back in my life, and I'd really like to keep her there.

As friends. Or more, if she were willing.

FOURTEEN

A loud pounding rattled the cabin, and Grace bolted upright in bed. Barkley plodded to the bedroom door, barking. She picked her phone up off the bedside table and checked the time—6:23 a.m. She had only slept about four hours. When Deputy Rice escorted her to the cabin a little before two, she'd found a note from Bridget's father, George Vincent, saying he'd stopped by and walked Barkley earlier, so she'd gone straight to bed.

The loud knocking came again. Jumping out of the bed, she quickly put her phone down and pulled on a long-sleeved Denver Broncos T-shirt and a pair of denim shorts.

Easing open the bedroom door, she started to tiptoe down the short hall. Then Barkley plowed into her, slamming her into the wall on his quest to get to the front door first.

"Ouch," she whispered as she rubbed the shoulder that had taken the brunt of the hit. She hoped whoever was at the door hadn't heard the bang.

Leaving all the lights off, she crept into the main living area and peeked out the curtain covering the window over the dining table. There was a white sedan parked in the drive. Who could it be? Her position didn't offer a clear view of the porch, but she could make out a man's silhouette.

"Open up, Grace," James's voice demanded through the door as he continued to pound on the solid wood surface.

Evan had only allowed her to return to the cabin alone because she had promised to stay inside and not open the door for anyone.

Barkley ran around and around in a circle, barking. He definitely wasn't good at being stealthy. The Great Dane's presence at the cabin didn't necessarily imply anyone else was there. Maybe James would leave.

She needed to call Evan. Quietly making her way back to the bedroom, Grace picked up her cell phone. No service.

The banging stopped, and James yelled, "Barkley! Down."

Barkley quieted. Grace inched back down the hall, pausing in the opening to the living area. The Great Dane lay down in front of the door, listening, his head tilted to the side.

"Grace, I know you're in there," James said into the silence. "If you can hear me, the hospital called. They couldn't reach you. Chloe—"

Grace flew across the room and fumbled with the lock, cutting off his words. Finally, she jerked the door open. James stood on the porch wearing a pair of black jeans, a white-and-gray-striped T-shirt and a lightweight gray jacket. He looked disheveled, his hair uncombed and his clothes wrinkled.

"What? What did the hospital say?"

James smiled. "Chloe is awake. She's asking for you."

"Why'd they call you? Why didn't they call me? Or Evan?" She eyed him suspiciously.

"They couldn't reach you." He arched an eyebrow. "I imagine you don't have the best cell service out here."

"Doesn't explain why they didn't call Evan." She looked at her phone. One bar. Not enough service to get a call out.

"Look. I don't know why they didn't call Evan. Maybe they tried, but he was busy. I don't know." James sounded aggravated, and he shoved a hand through his hair. "All I know is a nurse called and said Chloe was awake and asking for you."

"But why did they call you?"

He shrugged. "I guess Chloe never got around to changing her medical records, and I'm still listed as someone who's allowed to have access to her health information." Turning and heading off the porch, he added, "Look, I don't need the third degree. I came to take you to your sister. I thought it was one last act of kindness I could do before the divorce is finalized and I'm no longer a member of the family."

He reached the new, white sedan and opened the door.

"Wait!" There was no way of knowing how long Evan would be tied up at the station, and she didn't have a vehicle at the cabin. If Chloe was awake, Grace needed to get to her as soon as possible.

"Let me put my shoes on and take care of Barkley. I'll be right back."

Closing the door and locking it, she hurried to the bedroom, put on her sneakers and grabbed her bag. Then she rushed back into the living room and quickly filled Barkley's water and food bowls. "Be good, boy. I'll make sure Evan or someone comes by soon to let you out. Okay?" She rubbed him between the ears.

Time to leave Evan a note. Opening kitchen drawers, she hunted down a notepad and a pen. Bingo. The third drawer had a yellow legal pad and an assortment of pens and pencils. Grace removed what she needed and started to close the drawer when her eyes fell on a small cylinder. Mace. She bit her lower lip. It couldn't hurt to have some form of protection. What if they ran into Torres or his goon?

The door handle rattled. "Why did you lock the door? Let me in." James roared, rattling it even harder.

"Sorry. I'll be right there," she yelled.

Slipping the Mace into the front pocket of her shorts, she pulled the loose T-shirt down over it, concealing the weapon. Then, she quickly jotted a note for Evan.

> James came to get me. Chloe woke up. We're headed to the hospital. Please take care of Barkley until I return.

She paused. She'd almost written *Love, Grace.* Out of habit? Or because she had fallen for him again?

Her hand hovered in the air, her heart racing.

No need to sign the note, he'd know it was from her. But it seemed incomplete without a closing, so she wrote the date and time and her initials, like she would on a medical record.

Grace dropped the pen onto the table. Looping the bag over her shoulder, she headed out of the cabin, bumping into James, who stood glaring at her. "Why did you lock the door?"

"Habit, I guess." She shrugged and headed down the porch steps to the sedan.

"Where's your sports car? Did you trade it?" she asked as he held the passenger door open for her. She settled onto the leather seat, taking in the new car smell.

"Oh, um. No." He closed the door and jogged around the front of the vehicle to the driver's side.

Grace knew how much James loved his sports car. Chloe had said it was his most prized possession. "If you didn't trade your car, why are you driving this one?"

"The dealership loaned it to me. Uh, my car is in the shop." He shifted into gear and pulled around the cabin, taking an old, rutted logging trail, tree limbs scraping against the new vehicle.

"Why are you going this way? It's smoother to go out past the main house and down the drive." Was he trying to keep her departure a secret?

"This way is shorter." He glared at her. "Aren't you in a hurry to get to your sister?"

"Of course." She fought to keep alarm out of her voice. "I'd hate for you to get the loaner scratched on my account."

"Don't worry about it. I'll cover any damages," he snickered. "Getting to the hospital fast is the most important thing right now."

He barely slowed down when he reached the road, the tires spinning as he pulled onto the asphalt and sped away from Blackberry Falls, far exceeding the speed limit.

His behavior seemed reckless. The need to call or text Evan engulfed her. Slipping her phone out of her purse, she punched in his number. Nothing. *Don't panic.*

"Is your phone not working?" James nodded at the cup holder where his phone rested. "Use mine if you'd like."

Whew. He wasn't trying to isolate her or to keep her from telling anyone she was with him.

"Thank you." She picked up his phone and tried again. Nothing. What was going on?

"The cell towers could be experiencing an outage," James said as if he could read her mind.

"Maybe." She furrowed her brow. What were the odds of the cell service going out today of all days?

Evan wadded up the note. How had James found Grace? She should have been safe at the cabin. Had someone at the scene last night overheard him asking Deputy Rice to drop her off here? It would have only taken one person telling another where Grace was staying for news to spread quickly around town and into the ears of the one person they were fighting to protect her from. Once again, he'd failed a woman he loved. He slammed his fist on the table, causing the pen to bounce and roll onto the floor. Barkley yelped and took off to the bedroom to hide.

"Sorry, boy," he apologized to the Great Dane's retreating back.

Picking up the paper, he smoothed out the wrinkled note and reread Grace's message. According to the time she'd written, James had about a thirty-minute head start.

Evan barged out the door and hurried down the steps.

Wait a minute. How had James accessed the ranch unnoticed? The Vincents would have noticed an unauthorized vehicle entering and exiting through the main drive. A broken tree limb caught his attention.

Walking over to the area where the tree stood, he spotted tire tracks on an old, overgrown logging road. So that was how he'd done it.

Evan sprinted to his vehicle and followed the trail, his SUV bouncing over the uneven terrain. James must have been desperate to drive a rented sedan over a rutted-out logging trail. There was no way the vehicle wouldn't suffer some amount of body damage.

In his rush to leave the cabin, Evan had failed to check the guard duty roster to see which officer was at the hospital. He didn't want to stop long enough to pull up the email on his cell. Exiting the ranch onto the paved road, he hit the voice command button on the steering wheel and instructed the automated assistant to call Ryan.

His friend answered on the third ring. "Hi, Evan. What's up?"

"I'm driving and can't access my email. I need to know who's on guard duty at the hospital."

"The email wouldn't have helped you," Ryan replied. "Officer Nolan was supposed to be on duty, but he had car trouble, so Officer Wilkes came in his place."

"Okay, thanks—"

"Wait!" Ryan yelled before Evan disconnected. "What's going on? Did something happen?"

Evan quickly filled him in on the situation, including the information Marcia had shared with him. "If Chloe were awake, the hospital would have called me. They have strict orders to contact me if they can't reach Grace."

"I agree. It sounds like James used the only thing he could to lure Grace away from the cabin."

A new wave of guilt washed over him. "We must stop James before he reaches Chloe, but we've also got to keep him from hurting Grace."

"Uh…" Ryan paused for a second, as if struggling to find the right words. "Are you sure James is headed to the hospital? I mean Chloe's in a coma, and it's still unclear if she'll completely recover. Why risk going to the hospital at this point?"

Evan had been asking himself that same question since he'd first read the note, but it wasn't until this very moment that he figured out the answer. "Because he's meticulous and doesn't like losing. The person he relied on to take care of the situation failed. Then died. Now it's up to James to fix everything. Kind of like the adage, 'if you want something done right, do it yourself.' James's personality won't allow loose ends."

Muffled sounds echoed across the line, followed by the slam of a car door. "I'm headed to the hospital. I'll make sure a plan is in place. You just concentrate on getting here as quickly as possible."

"Are you sure? You can't have been home long after guarding Chloe last night."

"I'm sure. I'm only fifteen minutes away. Besides, there's no way I'd sleep knowing what was happening."

The weight on Evan's chest lifted ever so slightly, even though a panicked feeling of doom still lingered.

"Don't worry about things on this end," Ryan added when Evan remained silent. "If your timeline is correct, we have close to ninety minutes to head James off."

"Thanks, Ryan. Keep me posted."

"Will do." The line went dead.

Evan merged onto the interstate and accelerated well above the speed limit, racing to chisel away at the lead James had on him.

An hour later, there were only twenty miles between him and the hospital, and hopefully less between him and Grace. He couldn't imagine James would risk being stopped for speeding.

Evan itched to call Ryan but knew his friend was busy working out the security details and would call when he had a chance.

Traffic slowed ahead and then came to a halt. There was no sign of an accident, so he had no idea what had caused the standstill. Most likely it was a typical Denver traffic jam. He took a few deep breaths. Getting angry wouldn't help anything at the moment.

His cell phone rang, Ryan's number flashing on the

display screen. He pressed the answer button on the steering column.

"What's happening?" Evan demanded, unable to conceal the fear in his voice.

"As soon as we hung up, I called in a favor with Denver Memorial's CEO. He met me at the hospital, and we've spent the past hour putting a plan into place."

"Please tell me the hospital isn't surrounded with police cars and flashing lights. James will bolt if he suspects his plan has been jeopardized, and then we could lose Grace forever."

"Come on, give me more credit than that. I know we've not stayed in close contact in recent years, but I am good at my job," Ryan reprimanded him.

He dragged a hand over his face. "You're right. I'm sorry. It's so hard not being there, and now traffic is at a standstill."

"Where are you?"

Evan supplied the number for the exit less than half a mile away.

"Are you in the right-hand lane? Can you take the exit?"

"Yes." Turning on his lights and siren, Evan merged onto the shoulder and exited the interstate.

Following Ryan's directions, Evan was soon on a new route to the hospital. "Okay, fill me in on the plan."

"Well, like you pointed out, we don't want to alarm James or force a showdown in a crowded area, especially since we don't know if he's armed or not. Instead, security will alert us to his presence. Then when they arrive at the Neuro ICU, an undercover officer posing as a nurse will tell them Chloe was moved to a new room after she woke up. They'll be directed to a room on another floor where we'll be waiting."

"Sounds like you've got everything covered."

"We can't plan for every contingency, but we'll do our best to control the situation."

"Okay, well tell Wilkes to keep me posted." At least he had one officer on scene.

He needed to get to Denver Memorial to ensure Ryan's plan was carried out flawlessly. If it failed, Evan didn't know if his heart would ever fully recover. He pressed down harder on the accelerator, praying James and Grace were stalled in the gridlock on the interstate.

Grace checked her cell for what seemed like the hundredth time. Still no service. She sighed and dropped the mobile back into her bag. Stuck in a traffic jam on I-25, they had moved less than a hundred yards in the last twenty minutes.

Even though James was becoming more agitated by the minute, muttering under his breath and striking his hand against the steering wheel, for the first time in her life, Grace understood the term "deafening silence." There had been very few words passed between her and James since they'd left Blackberry Falls. She had tried to start a conversation a few times, but only received curt replies in response. James had never been one for small talk. Before long, the silence in the vehicle had zoomed right past uncomfortable to complete awkwardness.

What did one say to their sister's estranged husband? Now that she thought about it, Grace couldn't recall a single time in the three years of her sister's marriage where she'd had a conversation of any substance with her brother-in-law.

Since he didn't seem to want to talk, Grace used the time to have a lengthy conversation with God. First, she thanked Him for allowing Chloe to wake up, and asked for her sister's continued healing. Next she prayed for Evan and his emotional healing, from the trauma of his wife's murder and from his guilt for feeling like he'd let her down as a husband.

Dear Lord, Evan's a good man. Please, let him find love again. I know he'd be a good, caring husband, and he needs to realize it, too. And Camden needs siblings. He'd be such a good big brother.

A longing to be Camden's mom filled her. How had that little boy stolen her heart in such a short time? Because he was his father's child. A sharp pain stabbed her heart, and she caught her breath.

She loved Evan. Always had, always would.

If she had the slightest inkling he would give her a second chance, she'd move back to Blackberry Falls and take over the clinic. She could bear anything—even small-town living where everyone knew everyone else's business— to be with him. Only, small-town living hadn't seemed as much of a burden the past few days as she had believed it to be as a teenager. After hers and Chloe's attacks, the people had rallied behind her. The Vincents offering protection. The Greens providing a way into the match race, putting themselves at risk of retaliation. All the officers on the police force volunteering their time to keep Chloe safe so Grace wouldn't worry. She loved her hometown as much as she loved Evan. Reality hit her full-force, and she desperately wanted to hear his voice.

Digging in her bag, she pulled her phone out. Still nothing.

Maybe the guard outside Chloe's room could contact Evan for her. Who was on duty today? It didn't matter. Whoever it was, she was sure they'd help her out.

Traffic started moving, and soon James was speeding, maneuvering the rental car through the morning rush hour traffic, Grace's heart soaring with each passing mile. Turning to face James, she said, "Thank you for taking me to Chloe."

"My pleasure." The smile that tugged the corners of his lips didn't match the storm in his eyes. "It's only fitting I get to tell her goodbye."

The way he said the word "goodbye" sent a shiver of apprehension up her spine that wrapped around her chest and squeezed her heart. In that instant, she knew without a doubt she'd messed up by going with him. A sickening thought settled in her stomach like a dose of bitter reality. James wasn't taking her to Chloe out of kindness or a sense of family loyalty.

Maybe she was wrong. After all she'd been through the past few days, could she simply be chasing shadows in the dark? *Stay calm.*

"Goodbye?" She turned to study his profile. "Are you moving?"

"No."

"Oh." Grace tried not to sound disappointed, though she hated the idea of her sister running into her ex-husband and his girlfriend or, someday, his second wife, in the grocery store.

"I plan to keep working as a vet. In Blackberry Falls." James pushed his sleeves up, revealing a tattoo. A wolf inside a triangle, midway up his forearm.

Her breath caught. He was taking her to Chloe to kill them both. Grace had no idea how he intended to get past the guard, but she had no doubt he had a plan in place. James had always been a very methodical person. There was no way he hadn't considered all the contingencies.

She casually picked up her cell phone and tried Evan's number again.

"Have you not given up on getting a call through to

your boyfriend, yet?" James laughed. "Did you know you could buy a device that jams cell phone frequencies?"

That was why she didn't have service. And why James had offered her the use of his phone. He knew she couldn't make a call.

"You and Chloe both have the most expressive faces, making it so easy to read what you're thinking. I see you're finally starting to understand the situation."

No use denying the truth. "I believe so."

The sneer evolved into full-blown manic laughter.

Grace fidgeted with her hands, clenching and un-clenching her fists until his fit subsided.

"Why are you doing this?" she asked. "Is it because Chloe's divorcing you? Or because you're trying to cover up the fact you've been using the clinic to supply drugs to racehorses?"

He sobered and glared at her. "If it wasn't for me, Porter Animal Clinic wouldn't be the successful, thriving business it is today. Your father was a bleeding heart. I can't even begin to count the number of house calls he made without billing for the services. Or the number of ranch owners who had overdue accounts. And he never charged a late fee."

"I will not listen to you bad-mouth my father. He was a good man who tried his best to live by the Golden Rule."

"That *good man* was ungrateful and condescending. I brought in a lot of new clients—ones who never came in with sob stories to get out of paying—and even though I was married to his daughter, he planned to boot me out of the business. Said I was a sorry excuse for a vet."

"I never knew any of this."

"Yeah. Because he died in the car accident before he could tell anyone he'd fired me."

"You don't mean you…" She couldn't make herself say the words.

"Orchestrated his death? No. I didn't have anything to do with the accident." James smirked. "I just didn't try to save him when I happened upon the scene."

Grace gasped, tears stinging her eyes. Her fingers brushed against the canister of Mace in her pocket. Dare she use it right now? No. It would be too dangerous. She'd have to wait until they arrived at the hospital. Then she'd use it at the first opportunity.

"You might as well take it out of your pocket and give it to me."

"What?" she asked. He couldn't know she had a weapon.

"The Mace." He nodded toward her lap.

She glanced down and saw her shirt had ridden up, revealing the outline of the cylinder in her pocket.

"Did you think I wouldn't know what it was? Seriously, it's too big to be a tube of lipstick." He laughed. "Now, hand it to me and don't try anything funny. If you do, at this speed, you're guaranteed to take yourself out, too."

She pulled the Mace out of her pocket and deposited it into his outstretched hand.

"Good job, Amazing Grace," he guffawed.

Biting the inside of her cheek, she focused on the road ahead. She would not give him the satisfaction of acknowledging his use of her nickname.

They were about ten minutes away from the hospital. She'd been praying the entire ride a police officer wouldn't pull them over for speeding, keeping her from reaching Chloe as quickly as possible. Now, her prayer had shifted to the opposite. *Please, Lord, send someone to save me.*

James pulled across two lanes of traffic, barely avoiding being rear-ended by an 18-wheeler, and took the exit ramp.

"Don't try anything foolish," he commanded as he pulled into the Denver Memorial parking deck. "Or the deaths of innocent people will be on your head."

FIFTEEN

A feeling of déjà vu washed over Grace, her muscles taut and ready to spring out of the vehicle when it stopped. Four nights ago, she'd been in Evan's vehicle in a similar state of anxiety. The only difference was that this time she wouldn't sit and wait to be escorted into the building. When James stopped the vehicle, she planned to jump out and run with all her might. There was no way she'd placidly walk into the hospital with him, leading him to her sister.

He circled the first level of the deck and then took the ramp up to the second level, inching along in search of a parking spot. This was her chance. He was going so slowly, it wouldn't hurt too much to jump out. Right?

She wrapped her hand around the handle and pulled with all her might while pushing her shoulder against the door, but the door didn't budge. She tried again, James roaring with laughter in the background.

"Child safety locks are a wonderful invention, don't you think?" he asked as he pulled into a parking space and shifted the vehicle into Park.

Cutting the engine, he pulled a syringe out of the door pocket on the driver's side and turned to her. "I thought you'd like to see your sister, but if you can't behave, I can kill you now."

His face showed no emotion, his eyes cold as steel. "Well, what's it going to be? Do you want to get this over with and die here? Or would you like a little more time and a chance to say goodbye to Chloe?"

Her throat tightened and no words would form, striking fear in her that he'd take her nonresponse as agreement. Grace shook her head, finally managing to whisper, "I want to see Chloe."

"All right, then." James kept his eyes on her, the syringe still in his hand, while using his free hand to open the center console and remove a gun. "Now, you stay seated until I come around to let you out. If you try anything funny—like trying to escape or alert security—I will not hesitate to shoot you or anyone else in the area. Got it?"

She nodded, and her mind whirled. How was she going to get out of this mess?

"Dr. Porter, I'm so glad you're here." Evan heard the greeting through his earpiece. He was positioned in Room 1124 on the eleventh floor, and the female security guard posing as a nurse had just greeted Grace and James. Her words signaled that they had entered the reception area outside the Neuro ICU on the fourth floor. "Your sister is awake."

A gasp came over the earpiece.

"Really?" Grace asked at the same time James exclaimed, "What?"

"We tried to call but couldn't reach you," the undercover nurse replied.

"I've had horrible cell service today. But, um, we can wait to see her if the doctor needs to do scans and tests.

You know, to make sure she's okay." Hopefulness mingled with fear in Grace's voice, propelling Evan toward the door of the room where he waited.

Bridget put a hand on his arm and shook her head. "I know it's hard, but you can't go barreling into the situation. Trust the plan."

He bit back a retort, closed his eyes and let her words sink in. Rolling his shoulders, he took a deep breath and released it slowly, willing some of the tension to subside. Bridget was right. He needed his head in the game, not his heart. Evan would do more harm than good if he tried to storm the waiting area of the Neuro ICU.

He nodded and stepped back, forcing himself to focus on the words coming through the earpiece. What had he missed?

"So Chloe has made a full recovery?" James asked.

"Dr. Carson says she's going to be fine," the undercover nurse continued.

Though Dr. Carson had said these very words last night, Evan hated that Grace was being given false hope her sister had awoken and was headed for a complete recovery. He prayed, after everything was over, she would understand they had only lied to save her and Chloe.

"Well, let's go see her," James commanded as footsteps echoed over the earpiece.

"No, not that way," came the urgent reply. "Chloe has been moved out of Neuro ICU. Actually, you just missed her. We moved her into a regular room on the eleventh floor. I'll have an orderly show you the way."

"That won't be necessary," James said gruffly. "Just tell us the room number."

"No trouble. Oh, Mark, perfect timing. Can you take Dr. Porter and this gentleman to Chloe Osborne's room?"

"Sure, no problem."

"Mark is the orderly who transported your sister to her new room."

The orderly was actually one of Ryan's Protective Instincts employees. His job was to keep James and Grace in his sights at all times, ensuring James didn't detour from the carefully mapped-out plan.

"Really, there's no need. I'm sure Mark here has other duties he needs to see to," James insisted.

"No trouble at all," Mark answered. "This way, please." There was a ding, like the sound of elevator doors opening, and then muffled voices.

Ryan's voice broke through Evan's earpiece. "Okay, everyone. They're on the elevator."

From his position in the security office, watching the surveillance cameras, Ryan added, "We knew we couldn't control every scenario. Three other people were already on the elevator, and Mark wasn't able to prevent James from boarding. The elevator will stop on the seventh and ninth floors, but we won't allow it to stop on any others. I'm sending security to prevent other people from boarding."

Evan was impressed with Ryan's ability to get things done in a short amount of time. He really *was* good at his job, conducting the sting like a well-choreographed play with himself as the producer. Maybe one day, once this was all over and behind them, Evan could get his friend to explain how he'd pulled off such a large undertaking in less than two hours.

First, they had to save Grace. And save her they would, because Evan did not intend to spend another fifteen years without her in his life, even if it meant uprooting his and Camden's life and taking a job with the Denver PD. Or maybe he could get Ryan to give him a job at

Protective Instincts. He'd concentrate on that after they had taken James into custody.

"What does it look like in the elevator?" Evan had to know.

"James is standing in the back corner, holding Grace almost like a shield in front of him. I can't be sure, but I suspect he has a weapon of some sort in his pocket he's using to threaten her." Ryan continued, "Looks like the takedown will happen as planned."

The eleventh floor, part of a new addition to the hospital, was still under construction. On the surface it looked complete, with the hallways and common areas painted and the nurses' stations outfitted with filing cabinets and monitors. However, a look into one of the patient rooms, with its half-completed molding and no bed or wardrobe, would make it obvious the floor was not yet in use.

"Okay, folks, this is it," Ryan said over the earpiece. "All the other people are off the elevator. Next stop, eleventh floor."

"I guess they sent Officer Wilkes back home, huh?" James's voice sounded across the earpiece.

Evan was on full alert.

"No, sir. He's upstairs outside the room," Mark replied truthfully.

Evan had wanted his officer in on the takedown, so they had put a bodyguard from Protective Instincts outside Chloe's real room in the Neuro ICU.

"Why would he still be here?" James sounded incredulous. "The person who attacked Chloe was killed last night."

"I wouldn't know, sir," Mark replied.

Evan's mind whirled. How did James know who was on guard duty today? Especially since Wilkes hadn't even been on the schedule.

The elevator stopped with a slight jolt, and a ding announced their arrival as the doors opened. Grace stood rooted to the spot, her heart thrashing against her rib cage.

The orderly waved his hand toward the opening. "After you."

"No, you lead the way," James insisted. "We'll follow."

The man hesitated then met her eyes and smiled before he stepped out into the hall. If he knew he was leading her to her death, would he try to intervene? She opened her mouth, the words *Save me* desperate to escape, but closed it again. Grace would not be the cause of an innocent person being injured or possibly losing their life.

"Remember, don't try anything," James whispered into her ear before nudging her forward, the gun in his jacket pocket poking her back.

Grace nodded, her mouth too dry to form words. She followed the orderly down the hall, past the nurses' station where a lone male nurse was talking on the phone.

The eleventh floor seemed eerily quiet and there was a strong odor of paint and turpentine.

The orderly turned down the hall to the left of the nurses' station. A sign on the wall identified the hall as Eleven West. A man sat in a chair outside a room at the end of the long hallway. Officer Wilkes. Her heart soared at the sight of the familiar face. *Please, Lord, let him stop James.*

"Thank you for your help, Mark. We're fine on our own from here." James stopped, turned his back to the wall and pulled her to stand in front of him.

The orderly smiled and told them to have a good day as he turned to walk away, oblivious to Grace's struggle. She looked down the hall. Officer Wilkes stared in their direction. Could she alert him to the danger? She tried to signal him with her eyes, cocking them upward and to the side toward James like they always did in the movies. But the officer didn't budge. Maybe Evan was right. She watched too many whodunits. But, seriously, how could these people not see James was using her as a human shield?

Once the orderly had disappeared, James jerked her arm and led her down the hall toward her doom. As they drew closer, Officer Wilkes jerked his head ever so slightly at the door to room 1124. Was he trying to signal her? Was help inside? Her heart leaped.

Ten feet from their destination, James pulled the gun out of his pocket and put the barrel against the side of her head. "This is a setup."

Wilkes's eyes widened, and he jumped up from the chair, knocking it over with a clang. "Don't do anything foolish."

"Too late for that." James laughed. Walking backward, he pulled her through the door leading to the stairwell, the gun digging into her temple. Once inside, he raced up the stairs, dragging her behind him, his fingers biting into her upper arm.

"James, stop. Don't do this. Don't make things worse than they already are," Grace pleaded, but he continued on his mission, ignoring her appeals.

They were headed upward and had rounded the first landing when, below them, the door they had come through flew open.

Evan filled the doorway. "Stop, Osborne! Let Grace go!"

James's reply was a bullet fired in Evan's direction while still dragging her up the stairs. The bullet pinged off the metal railing and ricocheted, hitting the wall a few feet above Evan's head.

Grace screamed and stumbled, banging her shins against a step. James jerked her upward by her arm, and she cried out as a fiery-hot pain shot through her shoulder.

"No!" Evan yelled. "You could hit Grace."

Grace looked down and over the railing. Officer Wilkes and Bridget Vincent had followed Evan into the stairwell, and Wilkes had his gun pointed in their direction.

The trio raced up the steps behind them, and at each turn, James fired in their direction, slowing them down. Thankfully, he had terrible aim.

Please, Lord, don't let James hit anyone.

"Get down!" Evan shouted as a bullet whizzed past his ear. It was the fifth time James had fired at them as they followed him and Grace up the stairs. This time the bullet had come closer to its target. Even with his terrible aim, Evan knew, if he fired enough times, James was likely to hit somebody.

Without being close enough to identify the exact handgun James was using, Evan couldn't be sure how many bullets he had left.

"My men have arrived on the roof and are in position," Ryan said over the earpiece as Evan, Wilkes and Bridget rounded the last landing in time to see James drag Grace through the door.

"They just stepped out onto the roof. Tell your men to stay out of view," Evan commanded. "James has shot at us five times. I don't know how many bullets he has left, and I don't want him to use one on Grace if he feels pushed."

"Yeah, I was counting, too. I'll try to ID the gun when he steps into view of the security camera. Let's pray he didn't do his research and he only has six rounds."

"It's a Glock 42 with a seven-round capacity, if he put

one in the chamber and had six in the magazine," Wilkes said from behind Evan. "But I'm guessing he probably didn't know to put one in the chamber and then add an extra to the magazine, so he should only have one bullet left."

"How would you know?" Evan asked his officer.

The older man didn't reply, his face impassive.

Questions nagged at Evan's brain. Like how had Osborne known Wilkes was guarding Chloe today? And why had James suspected a setup after seeing Wilkes? Was it possible one of his officers—one who had showed him the ropes when he'd first joined the force as a rookie and who was only a few months away from retirement— could be corrupt?

"You need to go wait in the lobby, Wilkes. I'll talk to you once I'm done here."

"I can't do that. You need help rescuing Grace, and I need to know she's okay. I won't let you down. And I'll explain everything once Grace is safe and James is in custody."

"See that you do." Evan didn't like his officer having secrets, but he read sincerity in the man's eyes. He'd save judgment for later. Saving Grace was the priority right now.

"Okay, guys, we have them in our sights," Ryan said. "Grace looks okay, but she's holding her arm funny."

"I'm not surprised. Her arm made a sickening popping sound when he jerked her up the stairs earlier," Bridget chimed in. "Have a medic on standby, big bro. My guess is Grace's shoulder is either broken or dislocated."

Evan's gut tightened at the memory. "The longer we stand here chitchatting, the greater the chance she will be hurt a lot worse. Now, let's move."

The trio charged up the last rise of stairs. Bridget and

Wilkes had their weapons at the ready, having had them out since entering the stairwell. Evan pulled his service revolver from its holster and slowly opened the door. They stepped out into a small semi-enclosed area with a block wall obstructing their view of the roof.

"Ryan, tell your men no one shoots unless I give the okay," he instructed. Turning to Wilkes and Bridget, he added, "Stay out of sight. We don't want to agitate him."

Evan stepped out from behind the wall.

James was walking backward, facing him, while holding Grace tightly like a shield, the gun pressed to her head. "Don't come any closer."

"What's your plan?" Evan asked. "Do you expect me to provide you with an escape? Maybe a helicopter to take you far away?"

James smiled. "You're good at this, chief. That's exactly what I want."

There was no way Evan was going to let Grace out of his sight. Instinct told him the other man only had one bullet left otherwise he would have fired at Evan when he stepped into view on the rooftop. His only hope was to redirect James's focus onto himself, and maybe get him to release the last bullet, so Ryan's team could take him without a gunfire exchange.

"Remember, stay back," he whispered to his team as he took a tentative step forward, his eyes locked on James.

"I told you, don't come any closer." James pointed his gun at Evan, his hand visibly shaking.

Good, let him keep it pointed at me and not Grace.

Evan bent, placed his gun on the ground and then stood with both hands up, palms forward. "I only want to talk."

"If you want to talk to someone, get your phone out and call for the helicopter."

"I hate to say it, but I think you've been watching the same whodunit movies Grace has." Evan snickered.

"You think this is funny, Chief?" James tightened his grip on Grace and she winced, her arm dangling at her side. "Do you want me to kill your girlfriend in front of your eyes? Maybe seeing one woman you loved die wasn't enough for you."

Grace gasped, but Evan willed himself not to react and kept his focus on James. "You know, Osborne, you've always struck me as being very intelligent. There's no way you can think I'd send in a helicopter to whisk you away. But even if I did send one, do you really think I wouldn't have a trained law-enforcement officer on board to take you out?"

"Well then, I guess you signed her death warrant." James turned the gun back to Grace.

"You kill her, and you've signed yours." Evan forced himself to keep his tone even and matter-of-fact while he slowly inched forward.

James walked backward, getting closer to the edge. About four feet of rooftop and a three-foot-tall block wall was the only thing between Grace and the ground.

"Uh, Evan, we've got a problem," Ryan said in his earpiece. "There's an incoming medical transport helicopter that needs to land where you're standing. ETA four minutes. Or less."

He froze. James and Grace were standing on the edge of the landing pad, with Evan in the center. There was no way he was going to move back and put more distance between himself and Grace. But if he continued to move forward, James would keep moving closer to the edge.

Dear Lord, help me end this showdown without anyone getting hurt.

He forced air into his lungs and then puffed it out. "If someone has a clear shot, take it," he said under his breath, praying James couldn't hear but Ryan and his men could.

Grace continued to struggle against James's grip, fear etched on her face. Evan had to put a stop to this. Time was running out.

"James, turn yourself in. Don't make it worse," Evan pleaded. "There's an air ambulance helicopter coming. It needs to land—" he pointed to the helipad where they stood "—here."

"Well then, I guess they're going to have to land on top of us, aren't they?" James smirked.

"James, no. Stop this. They're bringing a criti—" Grace gasped as James dragged her backward by her injured arm.

"Yeah, then let's end this," he said, backing closer to the edge.

Evan rushed forward, and James turned the gun in his direction. "Don't make me kill you, too."

The whirling rotor noise of a helicopter sounded in the distance. James turned toward the sound, loosening his grip on Grace.

Evan watched, as if in slow motion, as she bent her arm, raised it and brought her elbow down on the inside of James's outstretched arm. His hand jerked upward, and the gun went off, the bullet shattering a floodlight on the side of the building.

Then she lifted her leg and brought her heel down on the top of her captor's foot. Caught by surprise, James lost his grip on her, and she ran as fast as she could in Evan's direction.

James straightened, lifting his gun and pointing it toward Grace's back.

Evan yelled, "Get down," but she couldn't hear him over the roar of the helicopter drawing nearer.

He reached behind his back and pulled his backup revolver from his waistband. But before he could get off a shot, a bright red circle appeared on James's chest, and he slumped to the ground.

Grace barreled into Evan, burying her head in his chest, tears soaking his shirt as a flurry of activity exploded around them. He slipped his arms under her, lifted her to his chest and ran to the stairwell. The helicopter hovered nearby, waiting to land, as a medical team and hospital security rushed to take care of James.

SIXTEEN

An hour later, Evan and Wilkes sat in a small room outside the surgical unit waiting area. The room, no larger than a broom closet with two hard-backed chairs, was a place for doctors to inform families how their loved ones did during surgery and what to expect for their recovery. In this case, Evan and his officer were waiting to hear if James had come through surgery.

Grace was asleep in the ER, one floor below them. Her shoulder had been dislocated and the doctor had given her a sedative before popping it back into place. She'd fallen asleep soon afterward, most likely from a combination of an adrenaline crash and the sedative. He'd left Bridget sitting with her, with strict orders to call him when she woke up.

He hated to be away from Grace even for a moment, but was glad for the opportunity to grill Wilkes about his connection to James.

"Let me get this straight." Evan leaned forward, elbows on his knees, as he studied Wilkes. "You've been working part-time as a bodyguard for James Osborne?"

"Yes, sir." Wilkes sat stoically, hands clasped and head bowed.

"How long has this been going on, and why didn't you tell me before?"

"He approached me a month ago. Said he owed this guy, Antonio Torres, some money, and he was getting threats because he hadn't been able to repay it. He said he only needed me for a month or two. Once his divorce was settled and the property divided, he'd be able to pay off Torres, and wouldn't need me any longer." Wilkes looked up, anguish in his eyes. "I didn't tell you or the other officers because I didn't want you to know I was having financial trouble, what with Martha's medical bills and all."

Wilkes's wife had been diagnosed with the onset of dementia a year ago, and he'd hired a nurse to stay with her while he worked. Evan felt instant remorse. He had checked on his officer's emotional health numerous times since the diagnosis, but he hadn't realized Wilkes might be struggling financially, too. Still, if there was the slightest possibility Wilkes had helped James with his plan to kill Chloe and Grace, there would have to be an internal investigation.

"Did you know he planned to kill Chloe and Grace?"

Wilkes gasped as if the words had slapped him. "No! I would have come to you immediately. I would never want either one of those girls hurt. Their daddy was a dear friend."

Evan hated to push further, but he had to know to proceed. "You didn't know his plan, but did you help him in any way?"

"Inadvertently, yes. He called to ask me to escort him home from the clinic Saturday afternoon. I told him I couldn't because I was at Mountain View Ranch with Dr. Porter." The older man's shoulders slumped. "I'm pretty sure that's how Avery knew where to find Grace."

"Anything else I need to know?"

"He called around five this morning to ask my availability for today. I told him I was headed to the hospital to cover Officer Nolan's shift because his vehicle wouldn't start."

"Which we now know was due to tampering. Johnson told me a few minutes ago someone had removed the fuel pump fuse from Nolan's car."

"Probably Osborne. He knew my work schedule, so he would have known I was off and would volunteer to come to the hospital in Nolan's place, especially since Martha is still in Albuquerque."

Wilkes met his gaze. "I'm sorry, sir. I only put two and two together when you came in this morning talking about Osborne bringing Grace to the hospital. I should have told you then, but I was afraid he would know it was a setup if he didn't see me."

"About that. How do you think he knew it was a setup?" Evan could not figure out where they'd gone wrong. He was eternally grateful that Grace was alive, but the scenario should have had a better ending.

"Well, sir. When you look at the video footage, you'll see Grace trying to signal me with her eyes—"

"I've told that woman she watches too many whodunits." Evan sighed.

Wilkes smiled for the first time since they'd taken off chasing James and Grace up the stairwell. "It took all my willpower not to burst out laughing, but I felt sorry for her, so I tilted my head and offered what I hoped was an encouraging smile." He sobered. "Only, Osborne looked at me and our eyes met and…" He bowed his head.

It pained Evan's heart to see his officer, and one-time mentor, looking so old and defeated. "I have to place you on administrative leave until an internal investigation has been conducted to make sure you didn't break any ethics rules."

"I know…and after the investigation is over, I'll retire."

"You don't have to do that."

"Yes, I do. It'll be for the best. I can be home to take care of Martha and spend time with her before she forgets who I am."

Evan's cell phone rang, and Agent Ingalls's number displayed on the screen. "Bradshaw here."

"I thought you'd like to know, we found Avery's phone in the wreckage. Antonio Torres tipped him off that when you left the diner, you turned in the opposite direction of the interstate."

"That's how he was able to find us. Avery had to have known I'd take that route back to Blackberry Falls." Evan sat up straighter. "Does this mean Torres is involved in the attacks on Chloe and Grace?"

"No. According to the text, the information was given as a means to clear up a debt Torres owed Avery. You don't have to worry about Torres any longer. The other reason I called was to let you know he's disappeared."

"What? When did this happen?"

"We've not been able to locate him since you and Grace saw him at the diner. The house where he was staying has been cleaned out." A heavy sigh sounded across the line. "Unfortunately, this is his standard MO. When he feels like the authorities are getting close, he closes up shop and goes into hiding. In a few months, he'll find a new location and start his operation up again. When he does, I'll be there."

"I'm sure you'll get him next time." There was a knock at the door. "Sorry, I've gotta go. Let me know if you ever need my help again."

Evan disconnected the call as Ryan entered the room, a somber expression on his face. "James Osborne died on the operating table."

The next morning, fumbling with the roll of masking tape, Grace slipped her thumbnail under the cut end, inched it along until she'd loosened a piece about three inches in length, and then used her teeth to tear the tan-colored tape. Success. Sliding the roll of adhesive into the sling supporting her right arm, she pulled the note announcing the clinic's temporary closure from under her arm and one-handedly taped it to the glass door at the entrance of the clinic. The note was hung crookedly, but it would do.

"Come on, Barkley," she called to the Great Dane lying on the floor in front of the receptionist desk as she headed for the stairs to the apartment.

She'd only taken a few steps when someone knocked on the glass door. Couldn't people read?

Grace turned. "I'm sorry, we're—"

Camden stood on the other side of the door grinning at her. "Grace, let me in."

Evan stood behind his son, a matching grin on his face and a picnic basket in his hand.

Unlocking the door, she stepped aside to let them enter. "What are you guys doing here so early?"

"We brought you breakfast. And flowers," Camden said, pulling a bunch of wildflowers triumphantly from behind his back. "Dad said you got a boo-boo and we needed to make you feel better." The child stared up at her with a hopeful expression on his face. "Did we?"

She smiled and knelt beside him, his eyes melting her heart. "Yes, you did."

He threw his arms around Grace's neck and she grimaced.

"Careful there, buddy. You don't want to hurt Grace's arm." Evan put his hand on his son's shoulder and pulled him back a little.

"I'm sorry. Did I hurt you?" Concern etched Camden's face.

"No." Grace shook her head. "I tell you what. Why don't you see if Barkley will follow you up to the apartment, and I'll let you feed him? Then we'll have breakfast."

"Oh, boy! Come on, Barkley, I'll race you!" The child took off running, laughter floating behind him as the Great Dane followed close behind.

Trying to stand, Grace wobbled and tilted backward. Evan dropped the basket onto the floor and rescued her, helping to steady her.

"Thank you."

"My pleasure," he murmured, his face so close she could smell the faint scent of his shaving cream.

Her eyes widened. "You shaved."

"If I recall, you once said you preferred me clean-shaved." He winked, turned and headed toward the stairs.

Her heart raced, and she fanned herself with her free hand. She had said that—when they were sixteen. He'd grown a mustache, and it had tickled when he kissed her.

"Are you coming?" he asked, smiling at her from the foot of the stairs.

If he continued to look at her like that, she'd follow him anywhere.

Thirty minutes later, Grace had eaten her fill of chocolate-chip muffins, fruit, and a ham-and-cheese quiche. "My dear Chief, I didn't realize you were such a superb chef."

Camden giggled. "Dad didn't cook. Grammy did."

"Hey, buddy, you're not supposed to tell your old man's secrets." Evan smiled and playfully tickled him while he squealed with delight.

A horn sounded outside. "Who could that be?" Grace asked, getting up to look out the window.

"Grammy's here!" Camden hugged Barkley. "Gotta go, boy. It's field trip day!"

She met Evan's laughing eyes as Camden gave her a side hug, being mindful of her arm in the sling, and bounded to the door leading to the outside stairs.

"I guess that answers your question. I'll walk Cam out then I'll be right back."

Evan opened the door and followed his son down the steps as she watched from the window.

After Evan retrieved Camden's backpack from his vehicle, he checked that his son was fastened into his booster seat. Then he kissed his mom's cheek, turned and headed back in Grace's direction. Pausing on the bottom step, he looked up at her with a smile and winked. He'd caught her staring.

Grace turned and busied herself clearing the breakfast dishes, a difficult task with her heart racing and one arm in a sling. Other than the ride back to Blackberry Falls, she and Evan hadn't been alone since she cried in his arms after escaping James. And she'd slept most of the way home after taking a pain pill the doctor had prescribed.

The door opened, and Evan came over to her, taking the plate out of her hand.

"I'll get this. You go rest on the couch."

Before she could protest, he turned and began loading the dishes into the dishwasher, whistling a tune as he worked.

Grace did as he suggested and settled on the couch. Tucking her feet under her, she pulled a lightweight floral-print throw across her lap, leaned her head against the cushion and closed her eyes. Her mind hummed with a myriad of thoughts. She had so much she needed to say to Evan. Could she string the words together into coherent thoughts? Was this how he'd felt on graduation day when he'd come to her, offering her his heart forever?

"Penny for them."

"What?" She opened her eyes to see him walking toward her.

"When I was younger, any time I looked deep in thought, Grandma Bradshaw would offer me a penny for my thoughts." He sat beside her on the couch, his smile reaching all the way to his eyes. "I always thought it was the funniest thing to say. But just now, seeing your brow furrowed, I suddenly realized I'd give much more than a penny to know what you're thinking."

"I was thinking how blessed I am. Yesterday, I didn't think I'd live to see today." She shrugged. "But here I am. I'm not going to take that for granted."

He took her hand in his. "Grace—"

Her cell phone rang, cutting off his words. Bridget Vincent's number flashed on the screen. Reaching for it, she slid her finger across the screen and hit the speaker button.

"She's awake, Grace! Chloe is awake!"

"What?" Grace looked at Evan. "I thought Dr. Carson wasn't going to try to bring her out of the coma for another day or two."

"I don't know what happened. Or why he changed his mind. All I know is I stopped by to visit, you know it kind of became a habit, seeing her every day, and..."

"Bridget, you're rambling," Evan interjected. "Does Chloe seem to be okay?"

"I'm sorry. Yes, she seems perfectly okay, other than a headache, but I guess that's normal. I mean she did sustain a bump on her head."

"Bridget, you're doing it again." Grace laughed, having a hard time rallying anger at the talkative girl. "Can you stay with Chloe until I get there?"

"Yes. Of course."

"Great, see you soon." She disconnected before Bridget could start rambling again. Then reality hit. "Oh. You weren't planning to drive me back to Denver until this afternoon. If you need to work this morn—"

"Nope. I'll take you as promised." He looked around. "Are your bags packed?"

"By the door." She nodded at the small overnight case she'd put there earlier.

He frowned. "What about the rest of your bags? I assumed you wouldn't be coming back for a while."

"Why would you think that?"

"Isn't that why you closed the clinic?"

"I closed the clinic because the doctor said I needed to wear this sling for three or four days. But also so I could go back to Denver to oversee my apartment being packed up."

"You're moving?"

"Yes. Back to Blackberry Falls."

His eyes widened, and she rushed on, needing to explain her change of heart. "The past five days have taught me this is where I belong. With people who love me enough to want to know everything going on in my life, so they know I'm okay. And when I'm not, I know they'll be there to pick me up and cheer me on."

"Are you sure you're okay with the *gossips* knowing all of your business?" he teased.

"I have lived in my apartment for ten years. Not one person in my building has a clue about the struggles I've been through. And if they did, they wouldn't care. They would think it wasn't their business." She nodded toward the basket on the table. "Your mom made me breakfast. Officer Wilkes has offered to mow Chloe's lawn, and Lieutenant Johnson is driving my vehicle to Denver so I'll have it to bring Chloe home. Oh, and Valerie is coming over in a little while to get Barkley so he can stay with her until Chloe and I get back."

"Have you forgiven Valerie?"

She recalled her friend's tearful phone call a few hours earlier. "Nothing to forgive. James manipulated her, like he did everyone else. He's the one who set her up with Avery Hebert, and he's also the one who told her I saw Avery's face when he attacked Chloe." Grace smiled. "Valerie is a friend, and I appreciate her desire to help me during this time."

"It's nice having people there for you. Helping you out and showing support."

She nodded. "Yes, that is nice. It's also nice being near the ones you love."

She bit her lower lip. Time to tell him. If he rejected her, she'd be okay, but she would never forgive herself if she didn't tell him what was in her heart.

She took his hand in hers, her eyes never leaving his. "I'm sorry I hurt you. That it took me fifteen years to realize how rare our love was."

"What are you saying?"

"I hope, now I'm moving home, you'll give me a second chance. And…" She took a deep breath.

"And?" His eyes twinkled.

"I know we can't rush things. I mean Camden has to get to know me. But I hope someday we can be more than friends again."

"Are you asking me to marry you?" He wasn't cutting her any slack, but she didn't care.

"Maybe someday I will."

"Why wait?"

"You don't even know anything about my life these last fifteen years."

"I know enough about who you are now to know I still love you. Nothing that happened will change that."

Her hands shook, and he squeezed them. "Evan Curtis Bradshaw, I love you, and I do not want to spend another minute of my life without you and Camden in it. Will you marry me?"

"I thought you'd never ask." He lowered his head and claimed her lips, and she knew she was finally home.

EPILOGUE

Five months later

"I can't do this!" Evan threw his hands up and stared at his reflection in the mirror. "Why did I let the salesman talk me into getting a self-tie bow tie?"

"Because, my friend, pre-tied bow ties look cheap and lack the elegance of a self-tie. And on your wedding day, it's important to look refined." Ryan laughed and turned Evan to face him, his fingers working quickly to complete the task at hand. "You're nervous, that's all."

"Nervous? I'm not nervous. I am ecstatic. This is the day I've dreamed of for half of my life." Evan caught a glimpse of Lisa's mom in the doorway, a sad smile on her face. He turned to her. "I'm sorry, Mom. I didn't mean that the way it sounded."

She smiled, tears glistening in her eyes. "I know."

Ryan quietly slipped out of the room, leaving them alone.

"Lisa loved you, and I know you loved her, too."

"I miss her," he acknowledged. "I will always miss her."

Sally Miller gave him a hug and then pulled back. "She would want you to be happy. So do her dad and I.

We can't bring her back, but promise me, you will keep her memory alive for Camden."

"Of course! And, since Grace's parents are deceased, both of us hope you and Dean will be grandparents to any brothers or sisters Cam might have one day."

A smile lit her face, and she placed a hand on his cheek. "We'd be honored." Wiping her eyes, she added, "I was afraid you'd get busy with your new family and forget us."

"You can't get rid of me that easy." Evan bent and kissed his mother-in-law's cheek. "I love you, Mom."

"It's time." Ryan entered the room, Camden and Barkley at his heels. The latter wore a special doggie bow tie that matched the ones the wedding party wore.

"I'll leave you guys and get to my seat," Sally said, bending to kiss Camden on the top of his head.

"Okay, guys, let's do this." Evan led the way out of the room to where the preacher waited.

The small group went down the hall and entered the front of the auditorium through a side door.

The decorations were simple and elegant. Candles flickered on the windowsills, and the pews were adorned with sprays of white flowers and greenery.

In spite of an early season snowstorm that deposited an unexpected eight inches of snow overnight, the small church where Evan and Grace's families had always worshiped was packed with friends, neighbors and loved ones.

The music began and Evan, with Ryan, Camden and Barkley at his side, turned to face the double doors his bride would walk through. The doors opened and Chloe, wearing a long navy blue gown, entered.

When she reached the stage, his soon-to-be sister-in-law smiled and whispered, "Wait until you see your bride."

A moment later, Evan's breath caught as Grace glided down the aisle toward him. She was wearing her mother's wedding dress, a flowing white gown with a beaded-lace bodice, her hair gathered into a low bun. Her face was beaming.

He met her at the foot of the stage, unable to take his eyes off her. "You. Look. Gorgeous."

She laughed. "What? This old thing?"

"I love you," they said in unison.

The preacher cleared his throat. "Would you two care to join me on the stage, so we can proceed with the ceremony?"

The audience laughed, and Evan offered his arm to Grace as they took the steps to their happily-ever-after.

* * * * *

Uncover the truth in thrilling stories of faith in the face of crime from Love Inspired Suspense.

Look for six new releases every month, available wherever Love Inspired Suspense books and ebooks are sold.

Find more great reads at www.LoveInspired.com

Dear Reader,

Thank you for reading my first Love Inspired Suspense. I hope you liked Grace and Evan's story. When we are faced with loss and difficult times, it's easy to lose faith and turn from God, like Evan did. Often, it takes another life-altering event to lead us back to God for the strength that only He can provide.

As I was writing this story, I knew Grace had to be a strong woman who had moments of vulnerability but would ultimately face danger with strength and, well, grace. I also knew Evan had to be a man of action who loved his family and his hometown, but who, being a widower, guarded his heart and didn't believe he deserved a happily-ever-after.

I would love to hear from you. Please connect with me at www.rhondastarnes.com or find me on Facebook @AuthorRhondaStarnes.

All my best,
Rhonda Starnes